Venice
Three

Venice Three

KEITH DEWHURST

GREENHEART PRESS

First published in Great Britain 2021
by Greenheart Press

Keith Dewhurst has asserted his moral right to be identified as author
of this Work in accordance with sections 77 and 78 of the Copyright,
Designs and Patents Act 1988

A CIP catalogue record for this book is available from the
British Library

ISBN 978-0-9571829-5-0

Produced by The Choir Press

Cover design by Paul Baker, A Stones Throw Design

KEITH DEWHURST was born in 1931 and worked in a cotton mill and as a travelling reporter with Manchester United before becoming a playwright. Three of his seventeen stage plays were premiered at the Royal Court Theatre and six, including his adaptation of Flora Thompson's 'Lark Rise', at the National Theatre. He wrote two movies, eighteen TV plays, of which 'Last Bus' won the Japan Prize, and episodes for many series, including the original 'Z-Cars'. He was a Guardian columnist, a member of the Production Board of the British Film Institute, Writer in Residence at the Western Australian Academy of Performing Arts and a presenter of TV arts programmes and a Granada comedy show. He has written two football books and co-wrote (with Jack Shepherd) a theatrical memoir.

Contents

To the serene Venetian state I'le goe
From her sage mouth fam'd Principles to know,
With her the Prudence of the Antients read
To teach my People in her steps to tread.

'Britannia and Rawleigh', attributed to Andrew Marvell

Lords of
The Night

SISTER ANNUNZIATA

When we take our vows we are supposed by the Rules of our Order to relinquish all worldly possessions, but because most of us are noblewomen this is, of course, impractical. Some leeway, to borrow a galley captain's phrase, lessens neither our piety nor our ability to do good works; and it demonstrates that our Republic of San Marco is as full of common sense as it is of hypocrisy and riches.

Nevertheless, as virgin brides of Our Lord and supposed poverty, we may neither bear nor suckle, and to numb the pain of this some have silk-covered cushions that when held to their breasts are pretend children. But I refuse to pity myself, and my new interest is this paper on which I write, my luxury from Egypt and beyond, that I have at last persuaded my brother-in-law to supply.

I confide to it my daily feelings and intend now to unravel at leisure a great mystery, of an unexplained woman and murders that took place fifty years ago, which is twenty before I was born. What this involves is the transcription and setting in order of a mess of torn parchments entrusted to me by an old man named Vico Pisani.

For centuries his family had known riches and importance, and they provided the Republic with two of its Doges. Their house on the Grand Canal was one of the finest, their galleys reached Byzantium and Tyre and Alexandria. Their younger sons were Admirals and their daughters made men rich with their dowries – which were often put to shrewder use. Over time bad luck and hesitant judgement, foolish loans and reckless borrowings were both the causes and the symptoms of decline. Vico's grandfather was the last to command even the amused respect of his fellow nobles, and when Vico's father died young, his mother struggled.

Who would marry such a widow with three children? Then the pride of the eldest son responded to a jibe, and he was killed in a street fight. His assailant was important, and escaped with a fine. Vico's mother sold the last part of the old house that she owned, two rooms at the back, but was allowed to pay rent to live in them with Vico and his sister.

Vico believed himself to be as good as anybody, and better than most, but in truth he was both small and lumbering. In his old age he had sweetness and a gentle eye, and even when he jumped to foolish conclusions he would laugh at himself later. He had the sadness of knowing his limitations, but being unable to address them, and I am sure that when he was young he was by turns insufferable and idealistic.

Because above all he meant well. Little that he did was for himself. It was for his mother, to restore her to what he believed she deserved, for his sister, to give her a dowry, and for the name and glory of the family. And caused by his shame and confusion, I realise, and the hurt that he tried to suppress.

Merchant nobles would not engage with him, because he had no money to invest, but when the Republic is at war it needs officers, and he was taken on for a minor affair against pirates in the Adriatic. In boarding a ship he was wounded, and never again had much use in his right arm; and it was despite this that through a last blessing of influence from his mother's second cousin he was elected one of the Lords of the Night – the street police, that is, who guard every district after dark.

This is the lowest form of service that one born noble can perform, because permanent posts in the bureaucracy are held by educated commoners. Nobles are elected for short terms to one supervisory role and then another, so that it is not individuals who wield power, but our class. Not that the Lords of the Night have much authority: what they see every day is more the hypocrisy of power and the unfairness of life, as in the case that begins Vico's story.

A poor man was killed, semi-accidentally, and the Republic did not care. Poor men have no value, and so long as they do not threaten good order little trouble is taken. But this case, as you will see, had for Vico a hidden temptation.

VICO PISANI

Pain in my wounded arm never did go away, and because salves and ointments were no help I turned to wine, and to the herbs that cause drowsiness. These did bring relief, particularly in the cold and wetter weather, when the spasms were worse. Wine fuddled me, of course, but I was aware of the fact and did not take risks. When I was on duty as a Lord I was extra careful, as on the night of the affray under a bridge where migrant workers slept.

Two or some said three Greeks tried to shove in among Ragusans. Tempers flared. One of the Greeks was stabbed, staggered into the canal, and drowned. Since I was hungover and it was a night with swirls of sleet I was true to my precautions and did not attend in person, but sent my patroller Giorgio. When he returned he said "We must talk. Get sober."

"I am sober."

"No you're not."

I am a noble and he was not, and he should not have spoken to me like that. But it can be the way of patrollers who are years on the job when we are elected for short terms. I also relied on him to cover up my absences on bad days.

In the alley he gestured with his chin. I scooped sleet crystals from the paving, and wiped my face. I gasped but the shock cleared my brain.

Giorgio held out a bedraggled purse. He pulled it open and spilled coins and a gold ring into the palm of his hand. He looked at me with meaning.

I inspected the ring. It had a signet and I recognised the emblem. The coins were gold, some Venetian and some Byzantine. They were worth more than a Greek drifter could earn in a decade.

"This was on the body?" I said.

He nodded.

"Who else saw it?"

"Nobody."

I waited.

"The other Greek ran off," he said.

"Which way?"

"Rialto."

Rialto. Once there he could have crossed the bridge or not.

"How do we know they were Greeks?" I said.

"Overheard talking the lingo."

"What about the Ragusans?"

"Ran the other way."

Foolish. Our district ended at the Custom House and the lagoon. If they didn't steal a boat we would catch them.

"Any witnesses?"

"A homeless woman. Sleeps in a doorway. Woken up by the fracas but didn't see it."

"No householders?"

"Same story. Woken up. Ran out. Body in the canal."

We watched each other. He had a square face and a lot of grizzle and his blue eyes were narrowed by years of knowing his place and keeping counsel.

"Want my advice?" he said.

I did. I always attempted too much. Or was it too little? I needed his advice.

"No clever bollocks," he said. "Investigate. Report. The rule book. We prosecute murders but we don't make the judgement."

It was true. All we were about really was order at street level, and above us there were layers of committees.

"Yes," I said, and went inside, where we did not have long to wait before our patrollers arrived with three live Ragusans and the body of a fourth. The three were jobbing oarsmen who had hoped to find a galley for the Adriatic, where they would jump ship and get home that way. The body was that of the oarsman who had actually killed the Greek.

When our men approached he had panicked, drawn his knife, and tried to fight them off. So they killed him.

"Bloody fool," said Giorgio, which was true. Our superiors would pronounce death for planned murder, but be lenient to the passions of a moment.

Had the oarsmen known the Greeks? No. So what happened? Confusion. One said that there were three Greeks and the others that there were two. But confusion. No sense to it. A bad dream. They woke up and their dead friend shouted and stabbed.

I believed them, and put them in the cells to await their transfer in daylight, which soon came, and with it our replacement watch; who were full of questions, having heard rumours, and peered at the Ragusans through the bars.

"We'll look for the other Greek," they said. "What about those taverns where the Greeks find girls? Why not start there? And while we're at it, we don't want these two bodies to stink us out. Usual arrangements?"

The sexton of the parish carted away such unknowns, and was paid a fee.

"Usual arrangements," said Giorgio. "We'll do the paperwork."

Outside he said "Did you tell them about the purse?"

"Of course I did," I lied.

"When?"

"When you were sorting them out at the cells."

He studied me.

"Was there another Greek?" I said. "And why run away? Why not stay to give evidence?"

"Maybe we'll find someone," said Giorgio, "and maybe we won't."

We were off-duty, and he would not discuss it. He bowed and left me.

SISTER ANNUNZIATA

Why am I in this Convent, you may ask. From a profound faith? A belief in the power of we who pray to bring good to the world? A need to be charitable? No. None of that. I am in a Convent because I am the youngest and plainest of four daughters. So it was easy for my family to decide that no-one would marry me, and to commit my future to the safety of the veil. A Convent demands a lesser dowry than a husband and that is why I am here. Not that young men have life all their way. Our nobility seeks to preserve itself at all costs, and younger sons often pay the price. To avoid daughters, and dowry money pouring out of the family enterprises, many young men never marry. This is why whores both great and degraded flourish in Venice, and why Vico's sister Barbara was unfortunate.

Convents are landowners and investors as well as prayer-houses, and will not take a noble like Barbara without a dowry, not even as a lay-sister, the ones who scrub, chop wood, dig vegetables and do the heavy washing for us of better blood. So Barbara found work where she could, like a common woman, and helped a tailor-furrier with his books, because unlike him she had been taught to read and write.

Why do I interrupt Vico's manuscript to explain this? Because he made here an omission that colours the whole.

Vico wrote that after he parted from the patroller Giorgio – who deferred to him because nobles are superior and must be seen to know best – he went at once to his benefactor Enrico Mocenigo, and struck the fatal bargain.

What he does not say, I think, is that first he must have gone home and rested. On his way, he would have bought millet bread instead of wheat, because it was cheaper, and his mother would have laid out cheese and wine as she always did when he returned from the night patrol, and over their breakfast Vico would tell her what had happened.

Who had done this and said that, and the decisions he had

made, and his smart replies to wrongdoers. His mother would laugh and praise him, and Barbara would rock her body, and steep her bread in the wine, as she herself was steeped in long-suffering silence.

Are we to believe that Vico did not tell his mother about the affray, and the purse, the coins and the signet ring? Loyalty to family is the Venetian noble's strongest motive, stronger in many ways than loyalty to the State. Vico's mother would have known at once that the ring that bore the Mocenigo signet implied a duty as well as a temptation. If her cousin Enrico was compromised, he should be helped and informed, as well as used.

Half their once-grand palazzo was a storehouse, and a carpenter occupied another floor, so that there was always rubbish in the back courtyard, and as they chewed in silence and mulled the situation they would have heard hammering and swearing, and working-class women shout at children: the indignity of their lives in the very air around them, as it were.

Did Vico then rest for a while, and smarten himself up? I'm sure he did, because I know what faced him.

Our government's appearance is one of grave committees that function with a seemingly selfless calm in every room of the ducal palace. The dirty business, the blackmail, the haggling, the buying and selling of power, is done elsewhere. And yet it is in public, and even in the open air: the famous broglio, where the Piazza San Marco opens into space between the ducal palace and the water.

There men pace and discuss, hover, form groups, re-assemble, laugh, touch elbows, salute acquaintances, bow gracefully to enemies. The scarlet or blue or purple or violet of their robes shows to what level of the government they have been elected, and the men not in service at the moment wear traditional black. All robes are trimmed, especially in winter: the furs of ermine, marten or lynx for the wealthiest, and of squirrel and lamb for others.

Vico, alas, had no robe of his own, but made do with one handed down from his father. It was worn, and the fur was straggly.

On patrol he would throw back his shoulders, wear an all-seasons cloak, wrap another round his bad arm as a shield, and carry a bludgeon that he sometimes shoved in miscreant faces. At the broglio he looked like a scarecrow. He was one of those whom other nobles call the sad ones, and would have been spotted at once.

But he was made to wait for half an hour, shuffling his feet, in sunshine but with a cold wind off the water, until a half nod summoned him.

VICO

"First and foremost," said second cousin Enrico, "how's your mother? How's Barbara? If only I had the time to help them."

He sighed, and gestured at the activity around us. Then he touched my fist, very gently.

"How is it?" he said. "How's your arm? Any improvement?"

I believed in his concern, because he had always helped me when he could.

I opened my fist, so that the purse lay in my palm.

Enrico pulled it open and saw what it contained. He removed the ring and slipped it on his finger, which he clicked at a man behind him, and said "Look at this, Manolis, what we hope for in families can come true. Signor Vico has worked and saved, haven't you, Vico, despite your misfortunes? Now he has a little money, which he asks to invest in our ventures."

Manolis was his Cretan clerk, morose and sallow, never impolite to me, but never warm.

"Signor permits?" he said, and took the coins. "If Signor attends the counting-house at the end of business I will have drawn the contract."

Their premises were on the route of my walk to the patrol post, but to make a show of confidence I had an oarsman land me at the canal entrance. The big ground floor was piled with goods and smelled of oils and spices and leather. Sandro, Enrico's third son, was the first person I met.

Sandro had commanded a ship already but he would never be as handsome as his father, nor have the same irresistible and trustworthy air.

From the time we were kids I never liked him. Mother said that he was the way he was because he had been ordered not to marry, and resented it. I just thought him conceited and sarcastic and as soon as he saw me he said "What happened to your hat, cousin? Been under water for twenty years?"

As a matter of fact it had been knocked off my head and into a stockpot when we made an arrest in an eating-house, but what I said was "Family heirloom, Sandro. Worn by Mark Antony at the Battle of Actium." Which I thought was a pretty smart response, and one which rubbed in the fact that my father's family was older than his. We were natural nobles, but Mocenigos purchased the right two hundred years ago.

Sandro grinned as though it was he who had taken the trick, nodded at my club and said "From what Concetta tells me your bludgeon isn't that big."

Concetta? He went with Concetta as well?

Manolis motioned from the side-room for me to sign the paper.

"So far as I'm aware," he said, "Signor has not as yet a trading structure of his own. Should we perhaps sell the goods on your behalf?"

"What commission?"

"Seven per cent."

"Two and a half."

"Five."

"Agreed."

Even if I were to re-invest half with them, which despite

11

having to endure meetings with Sandro I did, the profits would change my situation, and I had credit. The next day, for example, I ordered a hat, and a new fur collar and lining for my robe, and at the end of the month my mother engaged a skivvy, and invited me to think: should we start to save money to buy back half the palazzo, or should we look elsewhere?

At the time I continued to the patrol post. Giorgio was waiting and said "I'll leave last night's paperwork to you," which was the regulations anyway, but his way of telling me that I could mention the purse or not. It was up to me. At which my happy feeling stopped, my stomach lurched, and I thought: can I trust him? What should I do for him in return? Why have I embraced this at all?

I was re-filled with confidence when my report was accepted without comment and the Ragusans let off with a fine. This was taken from their wages, so that they rowed their way home but got nothing for it. Then the file was archived and the incident deemed trivial compared to one later in the week, when there was a scuffle in broad daylight between nobles who traded family insults and drew swords.

One man was run through the face, in one cheek and out the other. We were sent to find two assailants, of whom one resisted us. He slashed at my arm cloak with his dagger, Giorgio threw a wooden bucket at him, and in interrogation we established the cause of the quarrel.

We were commended for this, and I knew that my stock was rising. Later, I borrowed to invest again, in the mainland rice harvest, and when my patron Enrico was elected to the Committee of Ten, the most powerful body of state security, to whom our own superiors reported, he more than once invited me to the broglio. We paced with his arm through mine, and he asked me how things were at street level: how the patrollers judged things, and what our local traders thought about economic ups and downs.

"You know the government's problem," he explained. "Do

people tell us the truth, or do they tell us what they think we want to hear?"

This was in the last week of my six month tenure as a Lord of the Night and I duly asked the patrollers their opinions and wrote a final assessement.

Giorgio watched me sand the parchment and I knew what he thought. My report had mentioned neither the purse nor the ring and Enrico Mocenigo had neither explained nor asked another question, but had studied me at the broglio, I suppose, to see if I could hold my nerve. Something was wrong, knew our silence.

Out of it Giorgio said "Best say nothing to nobody about anything, then. Agreed?"

"Do you blame me?" I said.

He did, but said nothing. I felt bad, and I suppose I drank more heavily. But my mother dismissed all doubts. The money was our due, she said. It would make me the person I deserved to be, and amass a dowry for Barbara.

SISTER ANNUNZIATA

You will not by now be surprised to know that in my opinion Vico's mother was to blame for much of what he did. I have seen enough feminine plots within these holy walls, the most recent Sister Arcangela's attempts to poison my finches, not to know when – well, should Vico's mother have thought that to make Vico believe that he was cleverer than he was made up for his lack of education? She should not. Was his scrappy education her fault? Had she frittered money away?

Who knows? That she was opportunistic is clear. As clear as the fact that when his patrol responsibilities ended Vico would never be elected to a higher level of service, because he lacked the qualifications.

VICO

What the state values is age and experience. Its most important men are its oldest. So wait and see, I said to myself. Who cares that I don't have a legal training or experience of higher command? Anyway what did it matter? I had money, and was more respected. That's what matters, said my mother. The rest is just men showing off. What you should do next is seek a wife and a dowry.

"She thinks I should marry," I said to Concetta, who lived among the boat-builders' yards. It was noisy in the daytime but quiet at night. By this time I could have afforded a more expensive whore, but like Giorgio she was reliable.

"Marry?" she said. "Who?"

"Teresa Zampatti."

"Never heard of her."

"She's a widow," I said.

"Older than you?"

"Fifteen years."

"Ugly?"

"Very."

"Holy Mary."

"She owns a glassworks on Murano," I said. "It's cashflow."

SISTER ANNUNZIATA

Fifteen years was an understatement. Parish records show that Teresa was at least twenty years older, and other women had turned Vico down. Or, rather, their fathers rebuffed attempts at negotiation by Vico's mother. I know this because Sister Veronica whose cell is three doors down the corridor from mine, and who is too infirm now to attend Chapel, so that we sing every day outside her door, was one of them.

"My child," said her father. "Will you marry Vico Pisani or go into the Convent of the Blessed Eulalia?"

"Please, please," she replied, "In God's name, the Convent."

VICO

Of course, there is something about ugliness that is very sexy. It can be grateful, and in the dark, who sees it anyway? Teresa had her house on Murano and I soon realised the advantage of this. Oh, I thought myself a very smart devil, I can tell you, when my mother thought that I was with Teresa, and Teresa that I was with my mother, when in fact I was with Concetta; and sometimes not Concetta; and sometimes with none of them, but in the alleys and canal sides and the patrol post: dropping in as the old chum they were pleased to see, but actually in search of the answer.

Not that Giorgio was there to help. He had been wounded in an affray among fish and fruit stalls, men slashing and thrusting, the market women yelling, their displays scattered, a gush of blood across the white asparagus. I went to his house.

He was pale from the loss of blood, and the Jewish doctor had prescribed chicken broth.

"Trouble?" he said.

I shrugged. Life, I wanted to say. I don't understand it. I swagger one minute and feel stupid the next.

"Pity about your sword arm," he said. "You'd have been all set in the fighting services."

"I know," I said. "Obey orders. No need to think."

"Your family, though. Much more secure."

He was in pain but smiled at me, like an uncle who understands and forgives.

That evening I made such love to Teresa that she shouted and waved her arms and hair about and afterwards said "Isn't it about time you talked to me?"

"Eh?"

"It's my money," she said, "I deserve to know why you're a mess."

"It's not your money. You paid over a dowry and –"

"Shut up, Vico. Shut up and grow up."

She was kneeling on top of me. Her body was lovely, actually. Lumpy but lovely. She hit me in the chest.

"Why are you like this? Do you know what you say in your sleep?"

I couldn't believe it. She climbed off me. She was dismissive.

"Don't be like that," I said.

"I'm not your mother. And I'm not your Concetta, either."

"What?"

She did a mock groan at my uselessness. She knew about Concetta? How? What was I missing? What was I not noticing in the way people behaved?

"Cousin Enrico made a very generous speech at our wedding," I said, which to her was nonsense, but not to me.

She wiped sweat off herself. There were hairs on her pot belly. She put on her robe and whistled. Her kitchen boy appeared.

"Boil the clams," she said. "I'll start the sauce."

"Why did you marry me?" I said.

"Sex. You're young."

"You mean I'm attractive?"

"In the dark who cares?"

Moonlight. Daylit shutters. Braziers. Tallow flames. It wasn't always in the dark.

"Whereas you just wanted the money," she said. She had brought money to both her previous husbands. The second had been noble and started the glassworks.

"Of course you *are* a complete fool," she continued, "but there's something very sweet about you. So if we're to make the best of it tell me your troubles."

I told her.

At the end she said "I wish I didn't know any of that but I suppose it's better that I do."

A week later my mother said "You're not telling that woman what you used to tell me, are you?"

I wasn't sure which woman she meant, so I said "No." Women are all over us, I thought, like secret police.

Then I panicked, because Giorgio and I had agreed to speak to no-one. Could I trust Teresa? Why had I never spoken outright to cousin Enrico? What did Giorgio know but never tell me? What would happen if – ?

But it passed because I seemed to make money without even trying to and even stirrings in the big world did not worry me. Diplomacy was failing. There were those in Genoa who said make war on arrogant Venice and settle it, and those in our Senate who said make war on Genoa and settle it, and when we do we will be more prosperous.

So when war did start I approved the risk. It was in any case distant, engagements between ships on the far side of Italy, while I passed from one woman to another with a grin I tried to hide, and decided that we had enough to make a dowry for Barbara.

Mother said "I'll enquire about husbands," not trusting me to do it, I suppose, but what did that matter? I had provided for them, and it was the right thing.

SISTER ANNUNZIATA

What is of constant interest in Vico is his ability to shift his morality to suit himself: a constant balancing of lesser against greater evils in which Vico himself seems always to embody the lesser. To him this makes him worthy. Such reasoning is a sin of many people in this age, is it not, and in my experience it is most prevalent among people whose callings are to do with social standards. Joiners or boatmen, for instance, I find straight-forward. Educated people are not. Their notion of what is shameful can alter and – well, take Sister Arcangela and myself.

We are told that we have sinned and that our flesh must be

mortified, and we keep whips for the purpose. Sister Arcangela's scourges have cords of velvet, and she will bare her breasts and ask me to do the whipping. So far I have refused. This is why she tries to poison my finches.

VICO

Then some months later, and to my astonishment, I was in command of the patrol post again. The Lord of our district was called up to join the fleet sent to blockade Genoa itself and, as a wartime measure not to be held as a precedent, I was appointed without an election to be his temporary replacement.

Giorgio, recovered from his wound, was again my senior patroller, and we were occupied at once with the draft. The law was that in wartime one patroller in ten would be taken into the navy and there was bargaining, and offers of money, for older and unmarried men to take the place of those with new children or other worries.

We were in the middle of making one such an arrangement when young Alvaro Zeno, the Lord of the district next to ours, arrived unannounced at our post. After the handshakes, embraces and insincere jokes, he said that he would come to the point. He was thrilled at my re-appointment because my ideas were like his, he said, and he wanted to call a meeting about deterrence.

"Deterrence?"

Alvaro explained. He was picking up, he said, on what he had always considered to be one of my very good ideas. I was interested. He continued.

As we knew, his district contained the official business premises of numerous foreign nationalities who had the right to trade in Venice. Now numerous such merchants were stranded here by the war, and there was an epidemic of violence against them.

"Violence?"

Purse snatching, said Alvaro. Rowdy children would cause a distraction and deft men, and often women, would snatch the purse. It was difficult to stop because so few were caught in the act.

"But surely – "I began, and Alvaro said "Exactly." Genoa seemed to be drawing more states into an alliance against us. One of the last things we needed was for neutrals to be antagonised by opportunistic local crime.

We all knew the fences and hardened men who sat at home and organised the gangs. Martino Perago was the most important.

"He's in our district," I said.

"He sends his thieves into mine," said Alvaro, "and the fact is that the foreigners complain to the Council, the Council inform the Ten and the pressure ends up on me."

He wanted us to help him to set Martino up, which was not permitted, and illegal even in wartime. But he needed us, he said. He was worried that he could not control his situation. So we agreed, and made a plan.

When Alvaro had gone Giorgio said "It's you."

"Me?"

"The one he's actually set up."

I was furious with him but all I said was "We'll do what he suggests, and when."

SISTER ANNUNZIATA

Alvaro Zeno is old, now, of course, and has been the Doge of Venice for five years. He is agreeable, vulnerable-seeming, and unassailable. His political career has been a model. I assume that the patroller Giorgio realised from the outset that it would be, not least when he was told Alvaro's plan.

VICO

"Piero?" said Giorgio. "Martino's brother Piero? The sodomite?"

"The sodomite."

"Holy Mary."

Sodomy is a crime which the Republic punishes by death – by being burned alive, in fact – and it is within the jurisdiction of the Lords of the Night. It was understood, however, that we must never go out of our way to prosecute. If wider interests were threatened, yes. Otherwise let what was private be private.

SISTER ANNUNZIATA

Such Venetian pragmatism is called hypocrisy by outsiders. But in my opinion it is one of the reasons that our society endures. Another instance would be the behaviour of Sister Arcangela, and of others in our Convent, including rich girls placed here to be educated. Our sins are defined not by the State but by the laws of the Church. Which in Venice tends to deny that such things can happen at all.

VICO

If we stood at a certain point on the Zattere, not only were we about a hundred paces from the second-hand goods shop from which Martino conducted his affairs, but we could see a patroller with a flag whom Alvaro had stationed on a roof-top at the border of his district and ours.

Sunlight glared off the water, and we blinked and shaded our eyes, but it was unmistakeable when the man lifted the flag and waved it above his head. It meant that the fat sodomite brother, Piero, had a few moments before been arrested.

"You know what to do when you write this up, don't you?" said Giorgio.

Good God, I thought. He must think I've learned nothing.

"Information from, and acting at the request of . . ." he said. "If it goes wrong it was never your idea."

"It won't go wrong," I said, and entered the shop.

A phrase like 'den of thieves' makes people think of somewhere dark, dirty and frightening, but Martino's den was got up to please, in the style of a nobleman's quarters, except that it was higgledy-piggledy, everything was for sale, and very little had been top quality in the first place.

Martino lived on the floor above. He was a big man who wore caftans. He was surly but he always looked me straight in the eye. He had been a police informer for twenty years but we were always told not to rely on him.

He was haggling with a customer, saw us, gestured to say "A moment my lord," waved at an Arab boy to bring wine – did I say that he also bought and sold domestic slaves? – and turned his back. Giorgio said "He's put on weight since last week."

"It runs in the family," I said, and to show that we were in control strolled beyond Martino, and with an air of impatience.

The customer realised who we were, took fright, and scuttled out.

"Lord Vico," complained Martino, "that man was a shipper from Muscovy, and about to place a very large order to cash in on wartime shortages."

"What for?" said Giorgio. "Stolen horse-shit?"

"Cheap glassware," retorted Martino. "How's the factory, Lord Vico? How's the new Lady Vico?"

I started to compose a suitable put-down, caught Giorgio's eye, thought better of myself and said "I'll come to the point, Martino. The next district wants to torture that fat brother of yours."

"What?"

"A boy's mother made a complaint," said Giorgio.

"Boy? What boy?"

"If I mention her name you'll have her throat cut by this time tomorrow," said Giorgio.

"Look out for your own," said Martino. "It's full of phlegm that spits lies."

"Piero's been arrested," I said.

"Don't insult me. If he was arrested I'd know. Now what do you want?"

There was a din in the yard at the back. We knew what it meant and did not speak.

Martino looked this way and that. Then a man burst in. He was shouting, but stopped when he saw us.

"Please," I said. "Give your message."

The man twisted his cap in his hands and half bowed.

"Your brother," he said.

"Piero?"

"Arrested."

Martino picked something up and threw it at the floor. He realised that we had tricked him, but not yet how or why. We waited.

"I don't want him hurt," said Martino.

"Trust me," I said, and believed that he could.

At dusk we met Alvaro on the bridge that crossed the canal that was the boundary between our districts. We sat on the parapet and watched as a patroller fiddled with a flint. When the lantern was lit Alvaro said "Who would you say are the best torturers?"

I looked at Giorgio, who came up with some names, and said "Should I have a word?"

Alvaro shrugged and bobbed his head. He had a way of taking charge without seeming to do so, I realised.

Nobody asked him about the mother and boy who had made the complaint. Did they even exist as bought witnesses, Giorgio wondered later.

"How long will it take?" said Alvaro.

22

"Well …" I began. Statements from the accusers. Questions to Piero. Our reports to the Attorney, who had a month in which to bring a case. If the Attorneys considered Piero's replies to be inadequate, and asked us to torture him, all six Lords of the Night would have to agree. Then, put in Giorgio, there would be the usual argy-bargy with the torturers, about time off from their day jobs.

It could take a long time, which made Alvaro gloomy.

We reassured him. Don't worry, we said. We know our man.

Which is to say, we let Martino stew until at another dusk his door was ajar and tallow lamps lit, and his Arabs laid out huge cushions on which we sat, and accepted wine and roasted almonds and raisins.

There were more goods piled everywhere. "You can show receipts for all this?" I said, and Martino grimaced and made a businessman's gesture: tell me your concerns, it said, and so we did.

Assaults upon foreign merchants. Disorder. Damage to trade. The Republic's reputation, and its very safety in this time of war.

"Plus the minor matter," said Giorgio, "of us having got you by the balls."

So it was done. Martino called off his urchins for a few months and gave us the name of a rival fence, who Alvaro arrested. The Attorneys decided not to prosecute Piero, the mother being a mischievous informant, and two days after his release I came face to face with him in the vegetable market.

"Vico, darling!" he cried. "We've all been so worried about you!"

I was speechless. He wore gaudy clothes that made him look even fatter, and was arm in arm with a youth.

"I mean, webs are being spun all over you, Vico, and you don't know! But here's a little word because I love you …"

The youth giggled. He had a ferret under his arm, I realised.

Piero leaned as far forward as his belly allowed and with exaggerated lips mouthed "The runaway Greeks, dear! Ask at the sail shop! Not Greeks at all!"

"What?"

"Kiss, kiss, Vico! We're off to buy cherries for the little one!"

He must have meant the ferret, surmised Giorgio. But they'd have to stone the fruit, wouldn't they, he added.

SISTER ANNUNZIATA

Despite everything, as this encounter reveals, many people may have dismissed Vico but all sorts of them were fond of him. His grin was silly but infectious, and his blundering love for the women in his life was abundant. What he did was always for them, somehow, like a cat that brings home a dead bird, and he never realised that behind his back they must have talked to one another, and tried to protect him.

VICO

We sat on a stone bench in the little square off the canal that runs from the Grand Canal to the Zattere and the open sea. Behind us the church. Opposite, monastery walls rose from the water. Children played. A supply boat was poled along, barrels stacked, and a dog sat on top of them. Echoes of calls. Ripple and splash and autumn sun.

All ordinary. Yet the war was the shadow. What was the state of our battle fleet? To find out, what enemy would not pay to have a spy in the Arsenal's sail shop?

"Piero can't have meant that. Can he? How would he know? Has he told the Attorneys?"

"Thieves always know more than we think," said Giorgio.

"Giorgio, I said, "this is all airy-fairy. Say something solid."

He seemed reluctant. Then he said "Why did we think they were Greeks in the first place?"

"You said they were."

"I was told."

"Who by?"

"That street woman. All rags and no teeth. She slept in doorways."

I waited. I felt that everything had changed but I didn't know why.

"Fact is," said Giorgio, "that all she spoke was Venetian. Odd words of Tuscan Italian. Greek was Arabic for all she knew."

"The Ragusans said that they were Greeks."

"They said the dead man was."

"And there was one other or was it two?"

Giorgio stood. He's walking off, I thought. Then he turned.

"Things," he confessed. "Things I didn't tell you at the time."

"Didn't tell me?"

"You were too jittery."

"What things?"

"Next day. A man told a patroller that one of the Greek runaways was a woman."

"What?"

"Dressed as a man."

"What did the patroller do?"

"Nothing. Didn't believe him."

Cousin Enrico, I thought, telling me that government relied upon information but could never be sure that it was told the truth.

"Then later," said Giorgio, "people asked questions."

"People?"

"Not ours. Not local. I think," he said, and looked me hard in the eye, "that they were San Marco's."

He meant spies. Our Venetian spies. Or not. He waited. I wasn't sure how to answer. Were we in danger from them?

"Suppose we think about it as procedural," he said. "Suppose we'd found money in the purse, but no ring."

We would have made serious enquiries, such as: was the money the proceeds of a robbery?

"And if there was a ring with the money, but neither of us had recognised the signet?"

"The same. More so. Extensive enquiries."

Whose signet was it? Had a loss been reported? An assault? A robbery? Come to that, as regards the body, had anyone reported a missing person?

They had not, and there were no reports of robberies.

We reflected. Then Giorgio said "Was he surprised when you appeared at the broglio?" and we both knew who he meant.

I thought: was he? Was cousin Enrico surprised? Had he used the time he kept me waiting to gain information?

"I'm stupid, aren't I?" I said. "I blunder into things."

Giorgio said "Think of all the ways to get a ring."

"Buy it?"

"Borrow it."

"Steal it."

"Find it."

"Inheritance?"

"A wager."

"A gift."

"Which?"

"None of them," I said. "It could be a proof of identity."

You send a man on a mission. He is not known to your allies, but your ring is the proof of who he is, and of your good faith.

We knew the question but did not voice it. Why would Enrico send a man on a mission, and to whom?

"It could also," said Giorgio, "be the other way round."

"Other way round?"

"Your cousin Enrico wasn't the sender. He was the man sent to."

"Or his bloody awful son Sandro," I said, with a sort of insight.

"Or the bloody awful Sandro."

Behind us a bell tinkled. People knelt. A priest and his altar boy came from the church with the sacrament.

"Some poor sod dying," said Giorgio.

We made the sign, and I thought about the dead man in the water. What had he been? A courier? And how did fat Piero know things that we –?

Giorgio saw my mouth open to speak and said "No. No. We shouldn't ask anybody anything. What we should do is keep our mouths shut."

SISTER ANNUNZIATA

We think that we know war because we are told tales of heroes, but in truth we do not know until it happens to us, as we do not know about any catastrophe until it occurs. I realised this three days ago when our Reverend Mother Abbess joined us as we sang outside Sister Veronica's cell. She is a serene woman, who has served our community since before I entered it. But when we came in the chant to a moment of genuflection blood began to stream from her nose, to splash on the flagstones and drench her hands and habit. With other sisters I helped her away. After a while the bleeding stopped, and nothing has happened since; but she has lost her energy, and we fear that the worse will come. Our prayers seemed ineffective, as they must have been throughout the Republic, in the debacle of that shocking war with Genoa.

VICO

Meanwhile, in the midst of our concerns, pettifogging bureaucracy loaded us with distractions. War or no war, it demanded, where was our report on which connecting canals in our district needed to be dredged, and when would action be taken?

So a week or more was spent in skiffs and punts, or leaning over bridges, or hanging from walls with measuring rods, or hauling up unlikely obstructions such as a broken silk loom. Then a grappling hook found the corpse of a baby, not long dead we reckoned, weighed down with bricks inside an old sack. This invited a paperwork nightmare, and since it was found outside a convent, could well have become a scandal.

We decided to make a verbal report.

Before we had even sat down in their office on the ground floor of the ducal palace one of the Attorneys said "Could this be sensitive?"

"Very," I said.

They motioned us to the courtyard, where they ignored the legend that says that these walls in particular have ears, and asked me to summarise.

I did. They pondered. Then one said to the other "It's tidal there, isn't it? Stuff comes in and stuff goes out."

The other seemed not to know. He looked at Giorgio and said "Patroller?"

"Yes," said Giorgio. "Tidal."

They spoke together for a moment. Then one nodded at me.

"Have the body buried. Write your report. Our responsibility. We'll archive it. Well done."

SISTER ANNUNZIATA

The Convent referred to was, of course, this one. I have looked with discretion into our own archive, but no recorded deaths or disciplinary cases provide a connection. But one has known of comparable omissions.

VICO

Returning home from San Marco we faced each other on the thwarts of the skiff and were depressed by what the Attorneys had gossiped to us about the progress of the war. The oarsman was helped by a rising tide, and autumn's chill did not blow what we uttered his way.

"About before all this happened," I said. "I've remembered something."

"What?"

"Sandro said that my penis was very small."

"Sandro? Enrico's son?"

"Yes."

Comic consternation.

"This is vital wartime information?"

"He said that Concetta had told him."

"What?"

Then he realised.

"Yes," I said. "She thinks she never gossips but she does."

"You mean that maybe you told her things and that maybe she …?"

"Yes."

"And that's why someone asked questions about the Greeks?"

I nodded. It could explain why we'd been investigated but were safe, I hoped.

"Have you asked Concetta?"

"No."

"Why not?"

I gestured: who does ask whores about their other clients?

Giorgio was almost convinced. On the other hand there was Piero. But it could be that he had said what he should not, in order to mock us, and what he knew we would be wise to ignore.

"Anyway," I said, "I love her."

"You what?"

"Love her."

For what it's worth, I thought. For what it's worth, I do love her.

Our skiff reached the other side, and we scrambled out.

SISTER ANNUNZIATA

Mother Abbess has bled again, but inside herself. The pain in her head is excruciating, and she has a constant taste of blood in her throat. The physicians seem at a loss. One says that a devil has entered her, and she must be exorcised. Another, trained by Moors in Spain, says that there is a malignant growth. He gives her very little time to live, which raises thoughts of an election for her successor.

As you know, our abbesses are chosen for short terms in elections by secret ballot. These, whilst seeming to be orderly, are as hard fought between families and rival interests as are choices for the great offices of the Republic. Our Convent is like others a business enterprise after all, with its estates in the mainland, produce to be sold, and money to be invested.

Meanwhile we pray, and the exorcist is to come this evening.

VICO

One of Concetta's worst habits is that when she is excited she speaks with her mouth full.

"Whashyer mee …?" she said.

"Stop!"

"Nowonshop! Washyer …?"

"Concetta!"

She glared and chomped.

Even like this, she's comical and attractive, I thought.

"Shanro saysh … Sorry …"

Gulp. Swill of wine. Look for somewhere to spit it out. A

waving gesture which meant "Sorry not very lady-like." Then she spat and there was a patter into the canal below.

She inhaled deeply, turned, and said "Jacopo. That Jacopo. Conceited little sod."

"Jacopo?"

"Sandro's friend."

"Never heard of him."

"He was from Genoa."

"And he asked about me?"

"Once."

"When?"

"Can't remember."

I stared.

She was annoyed.

"Ago. You know. Ago. He was on the quay waiting to come in and saw you come out and said was that the one with the dead arm and I said 'Was it?' because I don't talk about people – and what's more, Vico, I never talk about bludgeons. I just tell everyone they've got the biggest I've ever seen."

She had told me that, I realised. Or was it *one* of the biggest? I was flustered but managed to persist.

"You mean you don't know Sandro himself?"

"I used to."

"Used to?"

"He dumped me. He can afford the fancy ones four doors down. They play lutes and sing."

"How do you know?"

"How do you think?"

"What else do they say?"

"Vico: I don't talk about people."

At this I could not complain. So I had better shut up, I thought, before she suspects that there is more to it than worry about the size of my penis.

This decision was correct, because she put her arm around me and said "It's really lovely that you're sensitive, Vico, but you mustn't let it get you down. D'you know what I mean?"

"Yes."

"Then give me a big wet kiss," she said.

Later, when we were on patrol, Giorgio said "Do you believe her?"

"Yes."

We turned the corner of the alley.

"Are you sure?"

I was, and we both realised what had happened, and that it tied Sandro to a Genoese.

"Local law and order," said Giorgio. "Don't pry beyond it."

But when I was forced to, it was not to be anything I expected.

SISTER ANNUNZIATA

Mother Abbess died last evening. There were no physical signs of devils after the exorcism, but she was calmer, and soon fell into heavy-breathing unconsciousness. Our corridors and parlour swarmed with people seeking to influence the election, but when Mother died they were asked to leave. Until we have voted we are forbidden contact with outsiders. My brother-in-law's opinion is that the peacefulness of Mother's end was due to opiates administered by the Moorish-trained physician.

VICO

"Has Concetta changed her hairstyle?" said Giorgio.

She had. It was the new rage among the courtesans: they washed and dried their hair in a way that made it frizzy, and stick out from their heads. As usual it would be talked about everywhere and respectable women, seeing their sinful sisters in church or on the canals, would be curious. After an interval they would try it themselves, whereupon the courtesans would discover something else.

"It's the war," said Giorgio. "Wars make people do crazy things like that."

SISTER ANNUNZIATA

Mother Abbess's death has disturbed me. Is God offended because we are lax in our observance? We must be, when for months I have failed to attend at least a couple of the day's offices. Now I am strict. Seven times I attend chapel, and seven times return on my knees, which are bruised and bleed a little. Last night, in the corridor between Compline and Matins, I slumped in a dizziness of exhaustion, and seemed to understand the meaning of Mother Abbess's life: its devotion, its strivings for purity and faith. I smiled with my eyes shut. Then I was aware of someone in front of me.

It was Sister Arcangela, her hands extended in supplication and her rosary dangling.

"God bless you, Annunziata," she said. "Help me in my penance, and in the election all my votes will be for you."

I was shocked.

"I do not wish to be put forward," I managed to say.

"My father has spoken to your brother-in-law," she said, "and told him that I need you to mentor me."

Your father needs finance, I thought but did not utter, to help him buy the forests on the mainland that supply the timber for ships, and my brother-in-law is a banker.

"I'm tired," I said, "and it's the middle of the night."

As she raised me by the elbow, and walked me to my cell, Arcangela leaned against me, and I felt the soft heat of her body.

VICO

After what the Attorneys had let slip about the state of the war I had concerns for how it might affect my wife Teresa, and visited her as soon as I could.

"This is ridiculous," I said. "I'm in the city with extra duties and you're stuck here in Murano. We'll never see each other."

"But when we do it's wonderful," she said. "You're the mysterious young man who fucks me and then leaves me to get on with things."

"Stay at my mother's until the war's over," I said.

"We can't rush about naked at your mother's."

Nor could we. So for weeks on end I did not see her. Then the weather worsened and our fears were realised. Disaster struck. Our fleet in the Adriatic was shattered. We were exposed. The Genoese arrived in the lagoon itself and besieged our southernmost territory. If it fell they could attack the city.

Our authorities were confused and desperate. I needed special permission to go to Murano, and could only do so on a patrol boat.

"You're not safe," I told Teresa. "They'll seize the outer islands first."

"I can't leave the factory."

Production had ceased, needless to say. There was no demand, and because of the blockade by Genoa's mainland allies, no raw material.

I was exasperated and waved my arms about. She changed the subject.

"How's Barbara? What happened to her husband?"

"Don't change the subject."

"What happened to him?"

"He isn't her husband."

"Not yet. What happened?"

He was noble but poor, and served as a naval officer.

"Was his ship in the battle?"

"Yes."

"Sunk?"

"Set on fire."

"No word?"

"Not yet."

"Did anyone escape?"

We didn't know. Barbara had been in tears for a week.

"At least you didn't pay the dowry yet," she said. "Or did you?"

"No."

She sighed. "Do you think I'm hard-hearted?"

I shrugged.

"Did you see the workshop at the end of the embankment?" said Teresa.

I had.

"They fled to the city. No sooner gone than the place was looted."

She was right. She had to stay.

I held her tight, my big, ugly, generous person. When she squeezed my buttocks in return I felt brave, and able to do my duty.

MOTHER ANNUNZIATA

By a complete majority of the votes cast in secret by members of the Chapter of our Convent I have been elected Mother Abbess for the next half decade. I am confused. I have prayed and wondered but not found much in my heart. My brother-in-law has sent in fine wines and sweetmeats. I have ordered them to be shared among everyone, which is to say that the lay sisters must not be ignored: without them our daily life cannot function.

VICO

In the city the mood was desperate. There had never been such panic and indecision. Above us the sky was grey and full of sleet and the smoke of the fighting blew up from the south. Indoors, the Great Council and the Committees bickered. On the street we received contradictory orders, but to tell the truth, they made little difference, because we were beset with problems.

Food became scarcer. There was looting and breaking into storehouses. People were afraid, and drank too much, and started fights. As street police we were always disliked by many. Now they were not afraid to show it, and our tasks were harder.

One of them was to ensure that the large numbers of men ordered to crew the hastily re-created navy actually turned up. Many of them had to be dragged from their homes, as their wives shouted and hit us.

And even as the churches were full of tearful people, the whores and courtesans did a roaring trade, and rough men treated them roughly. Concetta took in men of a sort that in good times she would never entertain; but they kicked at her door and abused her maid when she was sent out to try to find food. Then one man, a mercenary soldier, punched Concetta to the floor.

We found and arrested him, but the jails were full and empty warehouses had to be requisitioned. When the galleys were ready such prisoners were sent to be rowers.

I was panicky with worry for Concetta and for my mother and Barbara. I told them not to go out, and would take in what provisions I could.

Thankfully, in the last pre-war trade fleet to the Black Sea I had speculated in corn, and Enrico's warehouse held my store. It now commanded huge prices and what we did not sell or reserve we were able to barter for our personal foodstuffs: dried fish, and such vegetables as still came in.

So I was still lucky, and did not notice, I am afraid, how I had slipped once more into dependence on drink. It had been a friend when my arm hurt, and I persuaded myself that it helped me to think straight about the Greeks and the signet ring. But now I had to write a report of an incident of the night before, and I could not remember what had happened.

"It's not the first time, is it?" said Giorgio.

I admitted. No. It was not. There had been the men in the gondola. The woman in the spice shop. The colour of a cloak reported stolen. And –

"What?" said Giorgio.

"The man," I said. "The man."

"What man?"

We had been sent to help at a fire in another district. A man ran out of an abandoned workshop, and there was blood all over him.

"Injured?"

"I knew him," I said.

"Who was he?"

I didn't know. I couldn't remember. Had it even happened? Was it a nightmare, half retained?

"We were called to a fire," said Giorgio. "Three nights ago. It was chaos."

"Did you see a man?"

"There were dozens. Don't you remember?"

He stared at me. My effort to recall things was like a headache. I felt stupid, the way I used to be when I was younger.

"Anyway," I said, "what should we make up for this report?"

MOTHER ANNUNZIATA

Power, I realise, becomes me. I have spoken one by one to the Sisters whom I knew to dislike me, or suspect to have voted against me. I have invited their concerns, and will try to involve them in fulfilling works. We could well, for instance, open a school for orphans.

This will require not so much a dispensation from the Cardinal Patriarch at San Marco, as an indication of his goodwill.

To this end I have written to the Cardinal's confessor Father Baresi, a man of great influence, but whose knees are arthritic. It is difficult for him to get in and out of boats. So I have asked permission for me to go to him, when I will broach many matters.

Similarly, I expect my brother-in-law this afternoon. He thinks that my gratitude will offer him much of the Convent's money to invest. But my bargain will be in our favour.

VICO

At the height of the crisis sailors, shipyard workers and many marginal people rioted. They despised the government. They wanted the Admiral who had been imprisoned because he lost the Adriatic fleet to be released and reinstated to command the new patchwork navy, and they got their way.

Confidence returned, even if for no real reason. But the Admiral was vigorous and the Republic's other fleet, that had been active on the far side of Italy, returned in time, and it was the Genoese who were outnumbered and overwhelmed.

No sooner had this happened than Genoa's allies on land were defeated by our mercenaries: Germans and Swiss and Scots and unreliable French, whom the Republic's diplomats overpaid, so that they consented to play their part in the miracle, brought about by San Marco in heaven, that won the war.

Within weeks, it seemed, everything was normal and as it had been except that it was different. Our clothes were dirty, our boots in need of repair. Food reappeared but nobody seemed to know what to charge. On patrol, we were not sure of our new duties.

There were Masses sung, and processions, and Holy Relics paraded, because the Grand Council knew that it must do something to please people. At home, we accepted that Barbara's man was dead and would never return. I went to Murano to Teresa and was shocked: she had aged, somehow, and was much less interested in me.

Then one day Giorgio returned from delivering a prisoner to the Ducal Palace and said, "Heard the decision?"

"What?"

"Grand Council."

"You mean it's happened?"

"It's happened."

"Holy Mary."

For the first time in hundreds of years the Grand Council had voted to allow people to buy entry to the nobility, and hence a place in the governing class.

"People who lent money during the war," said Giorgio, "including you'll never guess who."

"Who?"

Well, for a start, Martino and Piero, the thief masters, the dealers in stolen goods and perhaps stolen secrets.

"Martino and Piero?"

"Piero."

"Piero …!"

We bumped into him hours later.

"Vico, darling! And faithful hound Giorgio! On patrol! Safeguarding us all, aren't you, darlings?"

He had his brand-new black robe already, and its ermine collar was fastened by a jewel.

MOTHER ANNUNZIATA

This week, hens are at the top of my agenda. Because we have two fast days a week in which we do not eat fish, but are each permitted two eggs, there is a constant demand, and our poultry are an essential resource. They also scatter into every nook and cranny. The reason for this, I think, is that every woman born needs an object of love to which she can devote herself.

Since Christ is an intangible presence, it is impossible to cosset Him, and besides, He is Our Lord and Saviour. So we have pets, or little possessions, on which we can lavish our unworthy silliness. Hence my own finches. Hence rabbits. Hence hens all over the place, shitting, shedding feathers, pecking and laying sometimes in unsuitable places.

To this situation I am determined to bring order. Birds must stay in their outside runs. Chicks may be indoors, in baskets, but not grown layers or capons being fattened for the table. Bird lime in chapel, on staircases and in corridors is offensive, after all. I have asked Sister Arcangela to organise this reform. As I said to my brother-in-law, if she had real power she would be dangerous.

VICO

One day Enrico summoned me to the broglio and confirmed that our district's Lord had been wounded at sea, and needed more time to recover. So I would be required to deputise until the spring. Then he asked me about Barbara. What was for the best? I wasn't sure. Enrico knew a childless widower, he said, who might welcome a wife to make his old age easy. He mentioned the name. It was a good one. Should we consider this in due course?

I was grateful, and said as much. Yet I knew from the way he studied me that there was more on his mind, and so it proved. He wanted to warn me, he said, about my drinking.

It had been noticed. There were doubts and questions.

"I'll do my best," I said. "I'll smarten up."

"I know how difficult it's been," he said.

"Yes."

"A word to the wise," he said.

"I promise," I said. "Thank you. I really will."

Alas, what Enrico called difficult was more than Barbara and her immovable grief. It was the death of Concetta, who never recovered from the fact that when the mercenary knocked her over with a blow to the face, she struck her head upon the floor. This, said the physicians, upset the balance of elements in her body, and caused her to see the visions which overpowered and killed her.

Concetta had been the one woman in my life with whom I felt so safe that I could be myself. She did not care that I was awkward, and so with her I was not. She was merry and loved pranks. She could sum people up, and always gave good advice. It was not calculated advice, like Enrico's, but words that made me happier and gave me confidence.

My wife Teresa did the same sometimes, but with her there was often some scheme at the back of it, some personal notion that she did not share. At the same time it was this separateness of spirit that I admired, and which excited me when we fornicated. I imagined that I possessed what actually I never could.

My promise to Enrico had been to "smarten up", by which I suppose I imagined that I would more or less not drink at all. I had achieved this after my first money-making successes but this time, with Concetta gone, I was too agitated, too confused, too angry and too sorrowful.

I knew that I must give the impression that I was trying, of course, and I managed to avoid extremes, which is to say that I did not binge but that I was on the edge, all the time, day and night, topped up, as the amused saying is. I chewed garlic to hide my breath. I relied on Giorgio, and could by myself make sense of very little.

Concetta's old maid Pia, grey-haired and heavy-shouldered, had been thrown out by their landlord, who wanted to put in another whore; but the boatyard men trusted her and made her their watch-woman, with a lean-to and a brazier outside.

This shed became a stopping-point on our midnight rounds, when I would stay and have Giorgio collect me on the way back.

41

Pia was angry and drinking herself. Her conversation rambled and sometimes I did not understand.

"What? Whatyoumean? What?"

"Wash a woman."

"Washerwoman?"

"No, no, no. You silly sod."

"Pia: what are we talking about?"

"Greek."

"Greek?"

"The Greek you never found?"

"Concetta told you about that?"

Pia gestured. Yes. No. I overheard. No. Yes. Anyway.

"What did she say?"

"Disappeared. Thin air. As easy as piss on your uncle."

It was what had puzzled me the most, I suppose. For all that it is crowded, Venice is surrounded by water and policed both day and night. Disappearance is never easy.

"Never sniffed nothing, did you?" said Pia.

"No."

"A woman, you see. Concetta knew a woman who was a man."

"A what?"

"Dressed as a man. Excitement. D'you get it?"

"You mean a whore?"

"No, no, no."

"Not a man in skirts?"

"You're not listening. Men's clothes. Turns some on. Expensive."

"What's expensive?"

"Came to the girls like a man. Paid them. Talked. Asked questions."

"What questions?"

"Well: women all want the same answers, don't they?"

She laughed at the way I must have looked, and started to mock me. I could not get her to talk sense. Then Giorgio arrived. I began to explain, stood, and fell over. He hooked me up by the elbow.

42

I shook him off. A woman. I must tell you.

"Not now."

He marched me along. I burbled. He halted.

"It's too late," he said. "Forget it. If they were spies from Genoa it's over."

I objected.

"It's another lost secret," he said. "Isn't the republic built on them?"

MOTHER ANNUNZIATA

Be aware. What Vico wrote now reveals that much of what he wrote before was not so much wrong or willy-nilly altered as somehow less than the truth; which is to say, the mercy that the mind shows to itself, and the knowledge it obscures. Was he convinced, for instance, that the Greeks who ran away were Sandro Mocenigo and the woman dressed as a man? Or was he ignorant, as I am ignorant about my body's desire for Sister Arcangela?

VICO

In no time at all, it seemed, Alvaro Zeno became one of the Attorneys to whom we were responsible. Despite his youth he was considered sound, and given the most difficult cases, such as the rape and murder of Ana Rovigo; which, thank God, had taken place in Tullio Grassi's district and not ours.

It was a dismaying case, and one that shamed us all, because for months nothing happened to solve it. Then it was given to Alvaro, and within days Tullio put in a request to apply torture. This required the approval of all six district heads, and gave Alvaro the excuse to call a meeting.

Ana Rovigo had been the daughter of a noble family that

owned vineyards on the mainland, and powerful interests in the galleys that exported wine to Flanders and to England. Ana was beautiful, people remembered, with long lustrous hair, a sharp mind, and a gift for enjoyment.

During the recent war, on the afternoon of what became one of those nights of riots and confusion, she had gone to visit an aunt and disappeared.

Her body was found two days later in the yard of a disused workshop. She had been raped, mutilated, and her throat cut.

An Attorney who held office before Alvaro wrote it off as an act of mob violence and revenge, of which there had been many instances, and some of Ana's family and most of the bureaucracy accepted this. Others did not, and among them was Tullio. He had plugged away but found nothing, which made him angry with himself.

"When you say that she disappeared," said Alvaro, as though he knew none of it, "what do you mean?"

"I mean disappeared."

"How?"

"There one moment and not the next," said Tullio.

"Where's *there*?" persisted Alvaro.

"The street."

Alvaro had the file.

"She was accompanied," he said.

"A maid and two armed house-slaves."

"They became separated?"

"There was a house fire. People rushing."

"Why wasn't she married?" said Alvaro. "She was twenty-one. Why wasn't she married?"

"Nobody could tell me," confessed Tullio.

"Betrothed?"

"No."

"Why not?"

"Maybe they were waiting for the war to end," said someone.

"Waiting?"

"Well. Rich girl. Big dowry. Big alliances. Take your time."

"Hmmm ..." said Alvaro.

Then without warning he looked me in the eye.

"Gut instinct?" he said.

"Something's wrong."

"Very. Very, very, wrong." And to Tullio: "Who d'you want to torture?"

"The maid and the slave," said Tullio.

Everyone looked.

"The burning building collapsed. The other slave was injured. Died a week later. It's in the file."

Silence.

"What would you propose?" said Alvaro.

Tullio glanced round.

"Fingernails," he said.

No-one responded.

"Why didn't you apply at the time?"

"No torturers. All at the war."

Alvaro sighed.

"It's true," said someone. "That man who flicked your eyes out was killed at Chioggia."

He had passed the trick on to his nephew, I knew from Giorgio, but did not say so.

I hated the case. The crime disgusted me. Yet how, now, could it ever be solved?

Alvaro gestured round the room. "Do you want to vote?" he said.

None of us did. Someone puffed his cheeks and blew out air, as though the whole thing was too uncomfortable. Assaults on noblewomen were unusual, and committed in our experience by jealous husbands or suitors thwarted in the battle for alliances.

"Thinking about all you've said," expanded Alvaro, although none of us had truly said anything, "will we ever find a culprit and make an example?"

No-one seemed to think that we would.

"In that case should we not ask the question: would it cause more grief to continue the case than to close it down for good?"

It would, said someone. It would cause more grief to continue.

There were grunted agreements.

"Close down?" said Alvaro. "Archive?"

Raised hands voted to close down and archive. And we could use the resources elsewhere, said someone.

Tullio was unhappy.

"Don't reproach yourself," said Alvaro. "If there was more to be found you'd have found it."

With mixed feelings we got up to go. In the shuffling and silence Alvaro said "Vico – a word."

I saw some of the others grin. Drunk again, they were thinking.

Then we were alone and Alvaro gestured. I had a flask up my sleeve and took a swig.

"Thanks," I said. "Sorry. I am stopping."

Alvaro shrugged.

"On the whole," he said, "I've led a very sheltered life. Aren't the Rovigo family related to your mother?"

They were. But they had dropped her soon after my father died, and we could no longer pretend.

"It's Ana herself, isn't it? Something about Ana. That's what the enquiry couldn't come up with."

I shrugged. Maybe. It was painful.

"Anything you remember?" he said. "Anything? I mean, from before the drink?"

I shook my head.

"There's nothing?" pressed Alvaro. "Or what there is you've forgotten?"

Forgotten? Forgotten the wonder of the years before my father died? Forgotten me and Barbara and Ana Rovigo as children? Forgotten when the girls tried to make the kittens friends with the cage birds? Forgotten being six and feeling big and brave like my father because Ana said "I don't care. I don't care what your

46

brother says. I think you're the best cup and ball player ever"? Forgotten later, when we were sweethearts and she kissed me? Forgotten how I felt before I knew I was ridiculous? Forgotten how her father discounted and laughed at me, and said that he would never allow her to marry me?

"Sometimes," I said, "I remember when I'm drunk, and when I'm sober I forget."

Alvaro smiled and gripped me by the shoulders, to encourage me.

"You've been good in this job," he said. "You'll be missed when your term's over. But you can't drink like you do and expect another government job, can you?"

No. I could not. Nor ever did.

MOTHER ANNUNZIATA

Arcangela oversees the construction of new hen houses. The young men from the Carpenters Guild who come in to do the work excite attention, and I have had to speak in private to three Sisters. But the Cardinal's confessor is impressed by the project, and repeats that other houses could well take note.

VICO

What did happen, after I ceased to be a Lord of the Night, was that our patron Enrico arranged the husband for my sister Barbara, and she accepted before she even met the man, going from tears one day to wild smiles and descriptions of how she would arrange her own household the next.

My mother was hurt, I think, and I was surprised, but Teresa said "Of course! Of course! She was glad to be free of you both!"

I disputed the "of course". In my opinion I had done my best for everyone, even when they were ungrateful.

"Done your best? Don't be ridiculous!"

"I've transformed all our lives."

"Pissed away my money, more like."

"Teresa!"

"The glassworks is in pieces but what do you care?"

"In pieces?"

"I explained."

Had she? Was I so drunk that I ignored it or did not remember?

She smiled at me and walked away. I followed, to put my arm around her. She shrugged me off. She sniffed and tried not to weep.

What had been between us was dead, I realised. I was angry. I jolted her to make her respond. She hit me in the chest with her elbow.

I tried to grab her with my bad arm, but was too awkward.

"Sod off," she said. "Stop it. Grow up."

"It's the war," I said. "It's done something to people. I don't know what but it has."

She was exasperated, and after a minute or two's silence I went away.

Some nights later a patrol found me passed out in an alley near the Arsenal. I had been robbed and beaten but remembered nothing. The men knew me and took me to my mother, but it was not long before Tullio himself found me covered in sick in a tied-up gondola.

"For pity's sake, Vico," he said, "for pity's sake."

He took me into a church and prayed with me. Candles shone on mosaic faces but it made no difference. God was not with me, I knew. He had turned away. I was a fool to tug at His robe.

A week later Enrico's man Manolis was sent to make the offer.

They would send me to Crete, to manage their outpost in a God-forsaken place called Loutro. They dealt in cheeses, wax, hides and honey.

"I don't know about cheeses," I said.

"There's a sort of clerk there," said Manolis.

"Sort of?"

"My aunt's cousin."

"I don't speak Greek."

"He has enough Venetian."

"I can't do it," I said. "I need the city."

"Signor may not remember," said Manolis, "but his mother has Greek, and is a most respected person."

"My mother – I mean, she can't – my mother –"

"Signor's mother has already agreed."

"To go to Crete?"

To Crete.

"My God. She'll die there."

He did not reply. I knew that I had little choice but to agree.

MOTHER ANNUNZIATA

People must be encouraged as well as disciplined. I gathered the nuns and novices who had been unseemly with the carpenters, and hired gondolas. We had an afternoon on the water that separates ourselves from the Giudecca. It was delightful, and a release of their energies. They were a flock of water birds, and when we returned it was to thank God with happier hearts.

VICO

Loutro – a shingle cove sheltered by cliffs atop which are the ruins of an ancient city. Its stones made up our meaner buildings. Enrico's warehouse was the biggest. Then two or three houses, pens for animals, vegetable patches, tamarisks, wild thyme, rowboats, heat, and sometimes the red dust of Africa blown across the sea.

On a nearby beach fresh water bubbled up through the stones, but we had to bring ours on the backs of mules and store it in jars. We were shut in by mountains, an idyll in summer and a misery in winter.

Twice a year galleys appeared, to and from Africa, and we would empty our warehouse. We lent the peasants money to buy sheep and goats and my mother became an expert judge of the cheeses. Indeed, it was she and not me who commanded our outpost.

Wrinkled by the sun, scrawny but energetic, she checked the books, doled out the money, weighed the fleeces, befriended the fishermen, ordered little luxuries from Tripoli and Alexandria, did not care that her clothes were patched and faded, learned the local songs and step-dances, and collected sea-worn stones. It was, she confided, the happiest time of her life.

Then one autumn day, after how many years I still do not remember, but when the galleys had left for Venice, she crumpled like rags and died.

I had to make another choice, I realised: to drown myself and my shame, or to be sober at last.

I put stones in a bag, held it to my chest, and walked into the transparent water. I stumbled. The bag held me down. The water was cold with the sun off it. I panicked. I choked. I threshed to free myself. I couldn't. Then I did. I broke the surface.

I was out of my depth and threshed again. I went to the bottom and scrabbled on my hands and knees, gasping, swallowing, retching, tearing myself on barnacles, and then I was in the air again and vomited.

People stared. I was an animal in the shallows. They were afraid to come near. When they did I waved them off. I was dizzy and I do not know how many days I endured, but perhaps they were not days. Perhaps they were nights, and the disconnected pieces of every dream I had dreamed, every ache and spasm I could imagine, and every memory I had lost.

Then I was awake. When I breathed the air was pure. It was clean, and so was I. Hollow cheeked I may have been, with grey all through my hair, but I saw everything afresh, as though I was a person in the first days of love.

And I knew that my mind-horrors were not dreams, but the memories that I had pretended never to possess. I knew everything. I knew who had killed Ana Rovigo, and why, and what I must do to avenge it.

MOTHER ANNUNZIATA

In a single night our herb garden has been ravaged. Urban foxes, claims the Head Spicer. But can there really be foxes on what are sandbanks made by men into islands? Arcangela, angel indeed, but of the dark, I sometimes think, says that the herbs have been stripped to make a potion that is guaranteed to procure an early miscarriage. This is a line of enquiry that, given the increasing goodwill of the Cardinal, I do not wish to pursue. But I suppose one must, in an oblique and sisterly way. Should we have admitted young carpenters to erect hen houses? Would an insistence upon older men have been shrewder? At least we can replant the herbs with a vigorous and more varied stock.

VICO

To return is to be shocked, to see a place anew, to realise again what is bad about it and what wonderful, before falling again into its routine. So Venice struck me. What an illusion it is, what a trick, the houses that float, the tall chimneys, the water-insect swarms of boats.

And ashore, what a stone brutality: the arrogance of the broglio and the men in robes, the din of the markets, and the alleys, damp and oppressive after the freedom of a beach.

I had sailed on a Bulgarian ship from Canea, and while she cleared Customs I mingled with the crew, to seem one of them.

Then when the sun set on black and yellow reflections I hailed a skiff and landed in what had been my own district, where I patrolled with power. But I could trust no-one, and speak to no-one, because no-one must know that I was there.

But I knew where to go to chance my luck – to the whorehouses near the boatyards. Pia and her brazier were long gone and as I loitered on the embankment the autumn wind cut across the water. I remembered those other nights, and my fantasies about myself, and I knew that I was not the same man.

I was a grey-haired little nobody with spindly arms and legs and a pot belly and I had only one ambition, which was to salve my conscience. I knew that I was not worldly-wise and for the most part not capable of reading people. I was a pawn in their games. I also knew my man, and I knew from experience how the law worked, both on the street and in the routines of the Ducal Palace.

Those odds I had calculated, and had trodden in my mind the path whose fork presents a choice of evils: and of sins, so that one meets either God or the Devil. God would be like an ideal Enrico, I thought, lined and angry, but forgiving, and his alter ego the Devil would be the Enrico of the broglio, sincere, perfect and smooth-shaven.

To be ready I slipped off my cloak and twirled it around my bad arm, to make the Lord of the Night shield. The dagger I held in my left, strong now after many years of use.

Will he remember, I thought. Will I have time to thrust across before he draws?

Then my stomach churned as I heard his voice.

He was behind me, coming from a whore's crib, shouting jokes over his shoulder, and unprepared because he carried his scabbard and belt in his right hand. He was bulkier, I thought, and more gross. I felt weak.

My mouth was dry. I tried to call his name, but before I could he saw me.

"What? Christ, not you? Vico? Never!"

"Ever," I said.

"What?"

"You killed her, Sandro," I said. "You're a lying bastard."

But my voice croaked. He did not seem to have heard me.

"Why aren't you in Crete? What's happened?"

"You killed my Ana," I said. "This is the revenge."

My cloak arm jutted to hold him off. He called for his man and tried to change hands on the scabbard.

I reached across and stabbed him. One. Two. Three. In the belly above the string of his hose, where his shirt was still open from whoring. It was easy, although there was resistance when on the last thrust I drew the blade sideways.

Guts and blood came out over my hand. Sandro fell forwards. Light splashed from the cribs. Sandro's man hissed and drew. Then I saw his brain working.

I was still a noble, and he was not. He would be punished more for killing me than I for killing my equal.

He decided to cover me with the blade, and shouted for people to call the patrol.

He did not even stop me when I reached down and slipped Sandro's sword from its scabbard, although I saw in his eyes that he knew that I was rigging the evidence.

I was exhausted but I kept hold of the dagger. When the patrol arrived the Lord was a young man I did not know, and Giorgio was at his side, older, gloomier, and somehow not surprised by what he saw.

MOTHER ANNUNZIATA

Mirrors are in every Convent a controversial and sometimes forbidden commodity. How Sister Arcangela comes to have one that is framed in gold and with a surround of semi-precious stones I do not know, but she has invited me to hold it at an angle and distance that will enable her to see her entire naked body. I have refused.

Is naked not how we came into the world, she asks. Would Christ not be pleased?

I refer her to a painting in the Order's possession of the Expulsion of Adam and Eve from the Garden of Eden.

She is meek, and suggests in a small voice that our School for Orphans be housed in permanence in a building across the canal. It is an excellent idea but we do not own the building.

Her additional notion seems to be that we engage an occasional singing master and develop the Orphanage as a Choir School. I delay. Our present Choir Mistress is old and infirm, I say. It would be kind not to hurt her feelings.

Sister Arcangela says that her father has secured a huge contract with the Arsenal, to supply the navy with timber.

This would make him the ideal benefactor, I think, to secure for the Orphanage and the Choir School the building across the canal. God does open doors.

VICO

There was much that I concealed in my interrogation, but at first only one lie. Sandro made a false and insulting reference to my sister's honour, I said. I lost my temper. We drew. I killed him.

"You admit that you killed him?"

"Yes."

The Lord, I saw, was not sure of himself. He glanced at Giorgio, but Giorgio did not look back. The Lord licked his lips.

"You had charge of a Mocenigo outpost in Crete?"

"I did."

"You left it with neither warning nor permission."

"My mother died. I was distraught …"

He waited.

"Nothing happens in winter," I said. "The clerk's there, and they could get a new man over the mountains in the spring."

He waited. What I said next was not even a lie.

"I went straight from the ship to inform Sandro of my return. You know how he greeted me."

"His man says he heard nothing of the sort. No explanations. No quarrel."

"His man was still joshing the whores," I said.

This was true, and the whores would confirm it.

"He also says that Sandro never drew."

"Well. The man wasn't much help to his master, was he? That's for sure."

The Lord agreed with me, I saw. At any rate, he let it pass.

"Why didn't you go to the counting house or your cousin Enrico?"

A tricky question. I needed a tricky answer.

"The counting house would have been shut. As for Signor Enrico, I – Well. What should I say? Sandro is – Sandro was my own generation."

"You hoped that he'd smooth things over? He'd make your unexpected return easier to understand?"

I did not reply. My silence made him think that this was the case. But he still had a trick up his sleeve.

"How did you know where to find Sandro?"

"I guessed. I was lucky ..."

He stared.

"He went with whores," I said. "Now that he's dead it's not ..."

I shrugged, as if to say, now that he's dead, let's remember what was good.

I looked the Lord in the eye. An appeal to his feelings. He nodded.

"You're not unknown, of course, Signor Vico. Your reputation and your previous service. So you know that we'll hold you in custody."

I did. I was beginning, for almost the first time in my life, to feel more intelligent than my surroundings.

The young Lord turned to Giorgio.

"Any questions, patroller?" he said.

"None," said Giorgio, staring at the wall.

The Lord seemed disappointed.

"How long will it take?" I said, to seem grateful. "Still a couple of months?"

"Or so," said the Lord. "No change there since you went away."

MOTHER ANNUNZIATA

When one is the leader it is difficult to have a confidante. I have taken to sitting with Sister Veronica, who cannot walk at all now. I hold her hand. For long minutes we are silent. Then she remembers old times, and I glean her advice by what seems to be similar gossip. I say things like "I heard a story about –" or "I once knew someone who –" or "Would you believe it but my cousin says –". The problems I describe are my own, of course, and the persons ones we know, but in this way do not have to be named. So I receive experienced, if sometimes rambling, comments, and they are of help to me.

Other questions I am not sure that I can ask her. How has she lived as a nun for so long? Did her carnal instincts wear themselves out? Has God truly been a physical presence for her? When we are put behind these walls for social and financial reasons, may a vocation not be hard to find?

These are questions that define my existence. Can I put them to my confessor? I doubt it. He is a man and for that reason I might not trust his answers.

VICO

Criminal examinations by the Lords of the Night are held every Friday between the Ninth Bell and Sunset. All six Lords must be present, and all concur, if torture is to be applied for: crushing of the head, say, or the extraction of nails. At the same time violence between nobles over matters of honour is frequent, and death as a result not unusual. So the degrees of punishment are well established.

Say a fight flares over something trivial. Three or four persons are involved and one is killed. The man who struck the fatal blow would expect to be fined, and then continue with his life. Pre-meditation, if proved, would be bad, and endangering the state worst of all.

But almost all pre-meditated murders are carried out by hired assassins. If caught these men are put to death. They are often citizens of other states, and a handful are skilled professionals known all over Italy. These would be expected to have arranged their escape, and never know capture.

Being aware of all this, I expected my examination to be a routine one. An insult to my sister would be an understood motive and my guilty plea accepted. A date would be set for an early trial. But it was not what happened.

The prosecuting Attorney was a frowning sort of man called Scisoni. He entered, sat down, and before he had even had the charge read looked around the room, stared at me, and said "Where's your lawyer?"

"I don't need one," I said. "I'm guilty."

"No, no, no. Totally irregular. Give him a list."

None of the Lords had one. We waited. When a clerk returned I jabbed a finger at the list and said "Him."

"Examination adjourned," said Scisoni, and walked out.

For six weeks nothing happened. Then one afternoon a skinny man who was all elbows and angles inside his cloak, huge eyes and a beaky nose, plonked himself on a stool outside the bars of my cell and said "Signor Vico? I'm your lawyer. Jacopo Barbarini."

The cell opposite contained Renzo Gritti, another noble, who had injured a shopkeeper in a quarrel over an unpaid bill. Now he clapped his hands and laughed and shouted "Jacopo! Not seen you since the Monsignor's funeral! How's your parrot?"

"Very fine," said Jacopo. "Anything you need?"

"Walnut cake," said Renzo.

"I'll tell your mother," promised Jacopo, and to me he whispered "Apologies for the delays. Tactical. What is all this? Why are they doing it?"

"Doing what?" I said. "You tell me."

"Taking statements. Examining people. Offering me a negotiation."

"A negotiation?"

His shrug flapped his gown. He was a busy little bird.

"You are who I think you are, aren't you?" I said. "You are the one whose uncle was the Doge?"

"No."

Holy Mary, I thought. Tripped myself up again. Even when sober.

"How's it been opposite Renzo?" enquired Jacopo, as though that was the purpose of his visit.

"He's moody," I said. "He sometimes sleeps badly."

"Well, his brother's the jolly one, after all," responded Jacopo.

His grin was crooked.

"And it wasn't my uncle," he said. "It was my father."

I felt safer again, even if I was a blunderer. I gave a silly grin.

He acknowledged it, as a schoolmaster would a clumsy pupil.

"Signor Vico," he said. "Everybody knows you. You were a so-so Lord of the Night, you hated Sandro and he hated you. Your wife was ridiculous and your life's a mess."

I objected to his description of me as a "so-so Lord."

"A so-so Lord and a routine case. So why is this Scisoni taking risks?"

"Risks?"

"He's told the Committee there's more to it. He'll risk his career, he says. Why would that be? Can you tell me?"

Should I speak? I didn't know. I stared at him.

Opposite us Renzo began to whistle: a sort of show-off

boredom: a sad tune that I wish I could forget but never can, because as we heard it Jacopo said "Who's Ana Rovigo?"

"What?"

"I know. You know. Scisoni says that he doesn't."

I spoke. I stopped. I tried again.

"It's in the archive," I managed.

"I read it. It wasn't even in your district."

"No."

He waited. I said nothing. How much could I trust him?

"Scisoni says that if you talk about Ana Rovigo he'll pursue it. Whatever happens you'll go free, he says. But that can't be in his power to guarantee, can it?"

His smile at this was as warm as it was unexpected. Then he tapped a bar of the cell, held a finger to his lips to warn me not to answer, and said "Scisoni's convinced that Ana Rovigo dressed as a man, and was mistaken for some Greek or other."

As he left he half turned to say "I'll come back the day after tomorrow," and Renzo cried "Walnut cake!" and changed his whistle to a jig.

MOTHER ANNUNZIATA

By now, whoever reads this will have guessed the reason for my interest. Vico gave me his papers because he discovered that my birth-name is Rovigo and that Ana was my father's aunt. As children, my siblings and I understood that she was murdered in a riot, when the last Genoese War created resentment against patricians. But no-one seemed to know much about her. "I was told that she changed," my mother would say, "and became very private." My oldest sister was told by a servant, however, that Ana had very long legs and would in secret wear a man's gaudy tights and doublet.

VICO

Jacopo did not return on the day he promised, but two later. He stood at the bars, said "This place stinks of shit," which it did, and paid the jailer money to let us walk under guard in the courtyard. I blinked a bit and must have looked dirty, and we were silent until I said "Parrot?"

"What? Oh! Woman client. Couldn't pay. Gave me a parrot."

"Is he green?"

"He is."

"Where from?"

"Oh, worlds away."

Jacopo had a cautious walk, I realised. He stepped tenderly, as though the pavings were hot.

"Made up your mind?" he said.

"Not really."

He did not seem surprised.

"I knew Ana as a child," I said. "Nothing after that until the case."

"Which wasn't in your district."

"No."

"Exactly," he said. No need to make a mind up, really.

After a few more paces he stopped.

"So far as anybody tells a defence lawyer anything," he said, "the Committees don't seem to be impressed by Scisoni. Old leaves. Why rake them over?"

The next day was a Friday. We had not expected to be summoned at such notice but we were, and as I was taken from the cells I glimpsed in a corridor the colours of important gowns, and Scisoni in the midst of them. He seemed reluctant to hear what was being said. One of the speakers, I thought, was Alvaro Zeno.

"Your client is aware," asked Scisoni as the Examination re-commenced after so many weeks, "that we can apply to have him tortured?"

60

Jacopo sighed, held his arms wide, and turned his saucer eyes upon the Lords, who did not want to look at him. He listed some Penal Statutes.

"To request the torture of a noble," he said, "implies either sodomy or treason: of which in this case there is no suggestion, no evidence, and no witness."

"Higher committees might find upon investigation," said Scisoni, "that behind it there are other crimes and events of interest."

He glared at the clerk to make sure that his words went into the record. But he did not add to them. He looked exhausted, and the Lords all looked away from him. He spoke again in a smaller voice.

"I am told that the trial can be brought forward and take place tomorrow. Would you be ready?"

We would. We pleaded guilty and I was sentenced as I had expected to a large fine, for which I had set aside the money, and to perpetual banishment from the Republic of Venice and any of her territories.

MOTHER ANNUNZIATA

How effective was banishment? For all our border controls, and all the Customs boats that cruise the islands and mainland waterways, how porous is Venice? Difficult to say. Harder for a known noble face to enter than for a common shipboard criminal, no doubt. But bear the question in mind, as Vico's story continues.

VICO

If I went to southern Germany, said Jacopo, it would be easier for him to arrange immediate bank transfers. I agreed, and he negotiated for me to travel with a company of mercenaries sent to relieve a garrison on the northern frontier.

My wife had refused to go to Crete and was dead now, but Barbara thrived. After I was arrested I had warned her to stay away and avoid implication, and my last acts in Venice were to entrust Jacopo with a keepsake for her, and to have him buy me a heavier cloak for the mountains.

Then two patrollers arrived to escort me across the water to Mestre. One of them was Giorgio. I was not surprised. Yet there was a glint in his eye that said wait: show nothing: there will be time. I was chained to him at the wrist, and on the customs boat we sat in silence.

At Mestre we found the infantry company and stood by the baggage wagon as Giorgio's mate and the officer checked the paperwork.

No-one could hear us and Giorgio said: "That man you saw at the fire when you were drunk. That was Sandro, right?"

"Sandro. He'd killed Ana in the building opposite."

"Why? To cover their traces? Make it look like a sex crime?"

"I don't know."

"Were they paid by Genoa? Was she involved? Dressed as a man? For the hell of it?"

"I don't know."

"I'm sorry," he said. "But I don't believe you."

"No."

Then he made his confession.

"It was me who went to San Marco," he said. "Told them about the ring. Before you even gave it to Enrico."

Of course he had. And I was never a smart one.

"It doesn't matter," I said.

"You loved her, didn't you?"

"Yes."

"But she was quicksilver."

"Yes."

"So she went with Sandro."

"I suppose," I said. "Until she realised."

"Realised?"

But he knew what I meant and we smiled at each other, remembering the years.

The officer yelled. We're ready to go. Giorgio unlocked me.

"Anyway," he said, and held out his unfettered fist. I opened my palm and he dropped something into it. I saw what it was.

"This? This can't be – who sent this?"

He had set off for the boat.

"Giorgio? What do you – ? What do they want? Giorgio! Who – ?"

MOTHER ANNUNZIATA

When I was a novice we would be sent out to hospitals and almshouses, to wash the feet of the dying, or to bring what gifts and charity we could. Vico still had a little money of his own, but lived in a foundation for old officers and captains of the Republic, and throughout his last winter I would see him every week or so.

He was not so much feeble, as very slow in his clumsiness, and restricted in movement. He said little, and seemed sunk in himself, and I suppose that we treated him as one of those old people who have lost their individuality, and are no longer interesting.

Then one day we were handing out scarves against the cold and he looked full at me and said "Your eyes. I've watched your eyes and the fleck in them."

I thought: this is not how a man should speak to a religious.

"I knew it before," he said, "in someone else."

"Indeed," I heard myself say, "and who was that?"

"Ana," he said. "She was called Ana Rovigo."

My start at the name made his eyes blaze.

"What?" he said. "What?"

His skin had death's whiteness, I realised, and out of that pity I told him.

Tears came and he tried to speak. Then a priest appeared.

"That parrot over there," said Vico, and the priest turned to look.

"Quick," said Vico. "Take this."

He gave me a bundle that I thought was a pillow.

"There's no parrot anywhere," said the priest, turning back, "but it's God's gift to the repentant: they are allowed a glimpse of paradise."

Then Vico died, with his eyes on mine, and since I was not supposed to have worldly goods I held the bundle as though it was something to do with the charity scarves. At the Convent I handed it to our Novice Mistress for safe-keeping, and the following spring, when I was a full member of the Order and slept not in a dormitory but my own cell, I reclaimed and opened it.

There were mementoes, long-dried crusts, olive stones, pebbles (I assume from Crete), a wooden platter, a spoon and various old coins, and a jumble of papers and vellum: business accounts, horoscopes, scrappy notes, and what I realised was a manuscript, written sometimes in Italian but mostly in Venetian, of which some pages were damaged, by salt water I suspect, and others missing – at the beginning and, most crucially, at the end.

This was Vico's story as I have transcribed it, and an immediate question would be how was he able to return to Venice, and where had he been during his banishment?

England seems to be the answer to the second part of the question, and his papers include the following draft of a letter, which he evidently wrote there. Above each letter is a number, as though this was the draft for encryption.

VICO'S ENGLISH DISPATCH

There is only one way to be sure that they do indeed spy on me, and that is to make an unexpected journey and see if they follow. They call themselves Milanese but I am sure that they are Florentines, and the English do not know the difference.

Southampton houses numerous foreigners, of course, because ships are holed up here for the winter – not least our own Venetian galley.

My friend the Lisbon pilot Master Geoffrey has a brother who is a monk in the big abbey on the Island, and I should go there, he says, accept their hospitality as a traveller, and see who follows. This I will do, and report the outcome in my next dispatch to you. The Bruges courier leaves as you know on Tuesdays, wind and weather permitting.

MOTHER ANNUNZIATA

Business accounts suggest that Vico was in Southampton as an agent for Venetians who bought English wool, which is the finest. Yet how could a criminal, exiled and in effect stripped of his citizenship, come to hold such a position? How in his old age could he re-appear in Venice, and be cared for in a public institution?

How could that have happened if he was not a servant of the secret state?

I have in my own life known one undoubted spy, and that was my father, who told me that before a voyage to Aigues-Mortes he was approached by a member of one of the Committees and advanced money to be given to Provencal merchants, as bribes for information. When I pondered this I realised that it could be applied in reverse.

I realised that the Genoese could well have enlisted Venetian nobles to give them information and perhaps, in the event of Genoese victory in the war, to be collaborators.

I realised also that Enrico Mocenigo may have been such a traitor, that one of his men may have been the Greek killed by accident, and that by returning the ring found upon the body Vico became an inadvertent problem. Seeking favours and family gain, he blundered into intrigues that were beyond him.

Then I remembered Giorgio the patroller, and his report to San Marco, and I saw that the sleeve of the robe could be turned inside-out. Enrico Mocenigo could be a Venetian spymaster who had corrupted the Genoese.

Or under pain of death he could have been the snake turned to sting his own Genoese employers.

Whatever he was, even after Sandro's murder he may not have dared harm Vico, but continued to help and make use of him.

And Ana. Our dead defiled Ana Rovigo who at night went out dressed as a man. Why did she change, and did Sandro kill her out of rage because after all she would not have him, or because – breathtaking question – she was San Marco's agent who monitored his treachery?

What I wrote twelve years ago stops there, as Vico's confession stops, because there was plague in that bad summer, and my duties diverted me. Now Arcangela is dead, my love, my darling, my burning body-mate, and my punishment is loneliness and wondering. I have served my term as Mother Superior. I am honoured because I doubled our Convent's prosperity, but in truth it was in economic good years, as I always admit to Sister Veronica. She is still alive, more than a hundred years old, and communicates by blinks and nods.

I devote to her the time that I spent once on the management of money and scandals – the latest of which is the smuggling into the Convent of inappropriate and even lewd romances in the Florentine manner.

I read them aloud to amuse Veronica. Her opinion, in the days when she could speak, was always that Enrico was the innocent father who protected his conceited son Sandro the traitor, and Vico the blunderer who wrote what he did to send to Barbara's late-born sons, but realised that he could not finish the story; that San Marco's alleyways are dark and in summer the canals stink and that what we must preserve is our Republic's security.

Who knows? What is definite is that he kept the ring, which was at the bottom of the bag he gave me. I hide it now on a neck-chain under my habit. It reminds me that before I became Annunziata I was another Ana Rovigo, and that although even within these walls I have had my adventures, they do not compare with hers: in the night world, dressed as a man, and risking the swordplay.

Day Pieces

Of all the Painter's frescoes the sequence in the Villa Braccio-Rovigo has provoked the most arguments among scholars. Its style is familiar: the rococo flowering of the tradition begun by Veronese, the lightness, the airiness, the ambition, the grandeur that in the turn of a glance, or a fall of drapery, becomes elegiac and melancholy. On ceilings and staircases the Painter would impose a single metaphor, and on walls a series of related, dramatized incidents; which is what he does in this case, to the left as you enter, ahead of you, and to your right. Then if you turn round there is the fresco to the left of the door, which is not matched on the right, and is of empyrean clouds through which a cabined gondola sways, and the ancient gods who watch are portraits. What does this mean, and why was it commissioned, and why is there no corresponding section? Who is the gondolier with the scar on his brow, and who are the boy, the jolly young woman, and the hollow-cheeked man portrayed as gods?

FRANCESCO CONTARO

He was not noble but like all the bureaucrats a citizen-by-birth, and his clothes were better than mine. He was young, newly promoted, and had the file and my letter on the desk. Since we had not met before he begged my forgiveness, but could he familiarise himself with the facts from the beginning?

"So when the Turks captured Crete your grandfather lost his estate and his life."

"Yes," I said.

"Your grandmother escaped with your mother, who was a babe-in-arms. Like many other penniless dependents they were settled here in Venice itself, and received a State Pension."

"Yes."

"In due course your mother married a much older man, your father Luca Contaro, who had also fled Crete when he was young, and was the sole survivor of his family."

"He was."

"When did he die?"

"When I was four."

He shuffled the file.

"I'm thirty-nine," I said.

"And have always received the Pension."

"Yes."

"You were never married."

"No."

For the truth is, who will marry a poor noble, except a similar?

"But you did once hold minor government posts?"

I shrugged. I have a variety of shrugs, each with its own implication.

"I'm a lobbyist," I said.

He decided not to pursue this.

"And now," he said, "your letter asks the State for an increase in your subvention."

"Changed circumstances," I said. "They necessitate higher outgoings."

He waited.

"I have a mistress."

"Right," he said, and wrote in the file.

"Rosa Ruggio," I said, and gave her father's address.

"She's not noble?"

"No."

"Will her family be embarrassed when we corroborate?"

"No."

He stared, was satisfied, and asked her occupation.

"Washerwoman."

His wig was too far forward, I realised.

'Washerwoman', he wrote, and asked "Where?"

I told him. He jarred his inkwell and had to sand a splash. I ignored it. He looked at me sideways, and in his eyes a memory flickered.

"Sorry," he said, "but are you the one who's the police spy?"

"Are you supposed to know?" I said.

"Wait," he said.

He spoke to someone in the corridor, returned, and offered me sherbet from a lidded bowl. He made small talk about a concert by the choir of one of the female orphanages, and asked if I had read in the gazettes the attacks upon the plays of Goldoni, and what did I think about this debate?

"I've not followed it," I said. "I'm more of a card player."

In fact I knew very well that Goldoni, like the younger painters, represents change, and that the people who attack him want things to stay the same. But sometimes it is better to seem ignorant.

A clerk appeared and said "Follow me, please," and I did, to a part of the Palace that for years I had wangled to enter, but never succeeded because the men with real power sneer at persons of my sort.

A bulky man whom I recognised at once came to meet me. He was Alessandro Perago, one of the three Advisers to the Council of Ten and the Doge. His family were ennobled for their valour in the War against Genoa, and have been important ever since.

He was wigless and shirt-sleeved. The undone buttons of his waistcoat had been Byzantine gold coins, I realised. His eyebrows were grey, his blue eyes themselves bloodshot.

"Signor Contaro," he said. "At last. Welcome. Let's walk up and down."

He clutched my elbow and said, "Don't worry about your letter. Similar requests have always been approved. But first –"

He swayed and stopped. He had a painful knee.

"But first," he repeated, "what's important is that you can help us find a missing person."

Missing? What did he mean? Who?

"Signor Antonio Rovigo," he said. "Where do you think he might be?"

THE REV HENRY ARDEN D.D. M.A. (OXON)

What I must iterate above all when I am sounded out by Mr Motcomb is that the Grand Tour, as we call it, is not an excursion for pleasure, no matter how many people treat it as such. No, it is a curriculum, through which a person leaves England a boy and returns a man, convinced by what he has seen in other countries that our British Constitution and manners are superior; and he is equipped by this knowledge to play his part in the upholding of them.

Other bear leaders may emphasise the arts and architecture as they are practised in Europe, or inspired by Classical examples, and I do not ignore this aspect, nor the controlled exposure of young men to sexual experience and hence the dangers of excess.

Indeed, I am known among patrons, and others of my profession, for my access in Venice above all to women of a tactful worldliness, as much as for my use of ancient texts to illuminate the journey.

Even that Irish scoundrel McSweeney – I will not call him Doctor for who knows whence the Doctorate came? – even McSweeney, when our paths cross in Geneva or Milan or elsewhere, will ask my opinion of intermediaries as often as, say, my reading of some passage in Suetonius.

And to be sure, some bears do return from the Continent none the wiser for their travels, and some with bad habits or the pox, which is –

Break off. Think better of it. Do not learn the above by heart except for the first paragraph. Deliver this in a slow voice, imply that it is Mr Motcomb's own view, and wait for him to ask questions.

Why, after so many years, and speaking to patrons as though it was for me to assess their suitability, and not they mine, do I need to write this to myself?

FRANCESCO CONTARO

"Holy Mary! Saints and Sinners! My arse! What?" said Rosa.

She has a powerful little body, and when she effs and blinds you would never guess that she can be as tidy as a cat. What a pickpocket she would have made, a patroller once said to me.

"What's wrong? Why are you staring?" she said. "Why are you scratching your balls? Don't say it's crabs again."

I love her deceits and evasions. They are a sexy excitement between us. But not this time.

"Antonio's great-uncle Braccio died two weeks ago," I repeated.

"So?"

"So Antonio's the heir. He's inherited the mainland estate. And San Marco need to talk to him. Urgently."

"So you said," she retorted. "If you want your balls scratched I'll do it for you."

"I'm scratching because you know all about it, don't you? You were as like as not there when Antonio got the news. Why haven't you told me?"

"You're the secret police."

After a fashion. More or less. To report on foreigners when requested.

"What's old Antonio afraid of?"

"Oh, come on, sweetheart!" she said, waving her arms.

If I'm the nobleman drowning in genteel poverty, I thought, why is it Antonio's life that passes before me?

"He was a very giggly and cheerful little boy," said Rosa, "but the fatter and more pop-eyed he got the more it depressed him."

"I know," I said. "Tell me. It got so bad he wouldn't leave the palazzo. Crouched against his mother, who put him in her old clothes and taught him sewing."

"Because she loved him."

"Because she was a very stupid and perverse –"

"It wasn't her fault she had to sell the palazzo," argued Rosa, who had been her laundry skivvy.

When his mother died Antonio wandered the alleys dressed as a woman, or hid in libraries, or more likely sought Rosa in the back rooms of her workplace, an illegal but tolerated male brothel called The Seraglio.

He relied on her. They gossiped and he did his needlework, and shelled peas and helped roll out the pasta.

San Marco knew some of this at least. I explained again what they wanted and said "So come on. Where is he?"

She took me, through alleys where one can lose sight of a person in an instant, and where Venetian nobles have long had their secret rooms, and their unexpected gardens on a canal.

She rapped a code on a door. Behind its grille a shutter opened. Rosa's face was near the grille.

The door was opened by a dumpy woman in a carnival half-mask.

"Oh fuck!" she said when she saw me, but I put my foot in the door and said "Come on, Antonio, don't be a fusser!"

"Really!" he said. "You two!"

He pulled off his wig and mask and offered his cheek to be kissed, and put his little arm around us both as best he could, and with his head buried between us mumbled something we could not hear.

"What about a biscuit, love, and a Vin Santo?" said Rosa.

He nodded. She fetched them and we talked.

"I don't trust them," he said. "That's why I'm hiding. They're all against me. They think I'm queer."

"No they don't"

"Yes they do."

"Well we don't," said Rosa. "I mean what's wrong with dressing like a woman?"

"A lady."

"A lady," she agreed.

"But I can't be a Magistrate in skirts, can I?" said Antonio.

He sniffed. He had wept, and his little red cheeks were wet.

"Signor Perago did brief me on that," I said. "It seems you

misunderstood. Your mother's uncle was the Magistrate, but it's not hereditary."

"Yes it is."

"No it isn't."

"It is."

"Your great-uncle tried to prove that it was, but for two hundred years it's been an appointment by San Marco."

"San Marco," said Rosa, and drained her glass, as though that was that.

"If you resign they can nominate someone else," I said.

Antonio began to speak but stopped.

My shrug said that to resign was the solution.

"On top of which," I continued, "your great-uncle wanted to preside over cases in which he was himself sueing people."

"Sueing people? What people? What for?"

"Goats, didn't Signor Perago say?" asked Rosa. "Other people's sheep and goats eating trees at the edge of his fields."

To my surprise Antonio knew what this meant. He was up and indignant.

"That's scandalous. That's our mulberry leaves. That's the food for our silkworms."

We looked at him. His mind had come together.

"Why didn't the lawyer tell me?" he demanded. "Can I trust him? What's happening? Holy Mary! I must go there at once!"

HENRY ARDEN

Never did an interview go better. Mr Motcomb has engaged me and at the same time given me fair warning of the assignment's difficulties. At an early stage in Tom's life an incident robbed him of his power of speech, and there ensued despair, alternating solitariness and dependence on his mother, bed wetting, which has now ceased, thank God, and recurrent bad dreams.

But if laryngeal paralysis is beyond cure, said Mr Motcomb,

Tom's spiritual and mental health are not. Might the sights and stimulations of the Tour not be restorative?

Is this hoping beyond hope? Time will tell. All I said, as boldly as I dared, is that in my experience the day a boy embarks upon the Tour is the day that his mother and childhood must perforce release him; many influences fade of their own accord, and others replace them.

He was bloody glad to hear that, said Mr Motcomb, a rough sort of dealer, who introduced me next to his wife.

Beneath her fragility there was steel, I thought, as she explained how it was always her ambition that Tom would grow up to manage her interests in Antigua, and then proceed, perhaps, to a broader life in England. Could a dumb person ever do this? What was the most that could be hoped for? Would the Tour inform us?

And Mrs Motcomb is gossiped about, of course, and it was her money, I believe, that enabled Mr Motcomb to buy his seat in Parliament, and I have now learned that she is the patroness of an excellent living outside Bristol.

Is this not the hope of every bear leader, to earn by his conduct some safety in his later years? Was my nervousness not fear of a difficult assignment, but serendipity, and has an eye been cast over me not just for tutor, but as the possible incumbent of a parish?

Mrs Motcomb's last question did nothing to dispel this view.

"Do you happen," she said, "to know a bear leader named Doctor McSweeney?"

"I do."

"Where does he stand in your estimation?"

I hesitated.

"Quite," she replied. "Quite so. We thought him deplorable."

FRANCESCO CONTARO

San Marco thanked me for my assistance in the matter of the Braccio inheritance, as they put it, and at the same time reminded me of the terms of the approved increase to my subvention: a noble's mistress must neither live in his house nor work, unless she is a paid courtesan or an actress or so forth.

Rosa was still a washerwoman. But it could continue, they said. It could be overlooked.

As I began to explain why, her own news interrupted.

"Antonio's gone," she said. "This morning. The mainland. He was very agitated. He'll catch them at it, he said."

How can a person be so scared one day and so reckless the next, I wondered, and said, "Them?"

"Overseers. Day labourers. The lawyers."

"Antonio can't run an estate that size," I said. "He's no experience."

"He knew about mulberry leaves."

I sighed. I thought that we had persuaded him to take time.

"Anyway. What about San Marco?"

I explained. They were bastards. They wanted her as a spy in The Seraglio, to add to their spies everywhere else.

"Why not?" said Rosa. "We can take the money and make up lies about foreigners."

That same evening, young Enzo's mother asked for my advice about his future.

ENZO

As everybody knows, one of the perks of being a gondolier like Dad is that you get into the operas free, so long as you cheer or hiss when they tell you. Our local cheerleader's a rower named Franco and he said "There's this castrato they want booed off. You can bring young Enzo if you like."

Was I excited? You bet I was, and Mum said "Go on then. Take him with you."

It was all candle-smoke, and people spat fruit stones on us from the boxes. We yelled and threw blown eggs full of our own piss and there was a riot, more or less, and I fell in love with it.

"I want to do it," I said.

"Sing? Don't be ridiculous."

I didn't mean sing. I meant the scenery. Make it. Paint it. Sultan's Harem. Shipwreck. Hermit's Cave. All that. Magic. Like when you look up in church and see the painted sky.

"Better for him than odd jobs in the boatyard," said Mum.

Dad never did think I had the build for a gondolier, so he asked Franco: do you know anybody backstage? Franco did. I was taken on by the scene-maker Marco, and it was great. Then a Frenchman who ran a theatre in Nancy offered the whole team more money to go to France.

"Their taste isn't ours," said Marco, "but we're better at the mechanics and so forth."

"He's too young," said Mum.

"It's how lads get on," said Marco.

"No."

I was gutted.

Marco saw it and said, "He's neat, though, and not stupid, and he can draw a bit. He'd be good on a scaffolding."

"Scaffolding?"

He explained.

Dad thought it was a great idea. Mum said, "How dangerous is it?"

But because she knew about the Painter she asked the advice of Signor Contaro, this noble who lives two floors up in our building, and he said "Go!" so she put on her best shawl to take me to the studio.

A watchful black man called Signor Nero was in charge and he said, "Why don't you help Cormorant while I talk to your mother?"

Cormorant had a beaky nose and was older than me and I helped him grind pigments. Real fun. Then he nudged me and they were in a line, watching. Mum, Signor Nero, and two men who looked alike, a father and a son.

The father was the Painter, of course. He seemed bored. Then he looked straight at me and it was as though he saw things that I never will and he said "Nero?"

"Cormorant?" said Nero, and Cormorant nodded.

"Good," said the Painter, and smiled at Mum.

Then Nero made an offer and I started the next day, and my nickname in the studio is Boatyard.

HENRY ARDEN

Preparations go forward. I have spent time with Tom and assessed his education so far. His knowledge of most subjects is patchy, but he learned to read before the paralysis, and communicates in writing. His spelling can be jumbled. He was never at school as such, but had tutors.

In appearance he has dark hair and a prominent mouth and in manner he is cautious and does not look me much in the eye. When he does there can be the most entrancing animation, and one is hard put to know how much of him is subdued, and why.

I discuss optimal routes with him and describe what we will see: the royal palaces of Paris, the Alpine glaciers and salt caverns, the ruins and great buildings of Rome.

His responses are muted, as he tries to decide whether he can trust me or not. Although at the mention of Pompeii he drew furious scrawls of an exploding mountain and wrote SENE IT!!!

Surely not, I thought. And then: was this the incident that shocked him? Or was it a dream, and is there an open frontier between his imagination and reality?

FRANCESCO CONTARO

As it happened young Enzo's first job was not to help erect a scaffolding, but to pull one down. He was excited that the ceiling was visible and Mother said "Oh, do let's go to see it!" although her eyesight is almost lost. All she sees are blurs with colours, and what she draws attention to are sounds, or silences when something is amiss.

Past Venetian noblewomen could not leave their homes except for church, escorted visits and public ceremonies. Today they go everywhere, even at night, but with their Walkers, platonic guardians who never leave their sides, not even for the toilette or the commode.

Mother is porcelain, but her Walker Signor Angelo is a massive man, in an ancient bottle-green coat, who tiptoes even as his voice booms, and he is a virtuoso of those niceties of the grand salons that we observe in our shabbiness, because they make our cramped lives civil.

Our rooms are tiny. When I am not with Rosa I sleep on a truckle at Mother's foot, although we always disrobe separately, and use different commodes. Our skivvy sleeps on the floor and carries water up from the courtyard, and slops and the commode pans down, and there are the other tenants, and musicians in the alley, and gondoliers at canal corners. We are surrounded by people. We share every stress of their lives. Why would the breeze off the water not refresh us as we walked?

Signor Angelo held Mother's lace-gloved hand (patching and darning in tallow light was a reason her eyes had gone) at shoulder height: elegant in a dance and helpful if she stumbled, and I had her other elbow.

In the church there was dust and confusion as they took their poles and planks out to a scow. I had hoped to meet the Painter and his son but they had left their factotum Signor Nero in charge, and Mother asked him if Enzo might describe the fresco to her. He was pleased to let Enzo do so, and Signor Angelo, whose fiction is that he's compiling a history of our Venetian Crete, put in learned-seeming observations.

Angelo's life is empty, Mother says, and he needs imaginary work to fill it.

Then on the stroll home she said in an off-hand way that two rooms are coming vacant at the back of the floor above us. Would it be regarded as a separate dwelling? If so we could put Rosa there and she would be as good as with us.

That they had taken to each other was my best fortune.

"But what compromises," sighed Mother, "and how we have become used to them."

We were silent. Then she stopped and felt my cuffs and lapels.

"I'm right, aren't I, Angelo?" she said. "He's threadbare."

I was, and my shoes worn at the heels.

"Three lots of money coming in," said Mother. "Have a new coat made."

Angelo suggested a tailor who gives credit. Compared to others we are lucky, despite everything.

Next day there came a message from Antonio's mainland lawyer.

HENRY ARDEN

On former Tours I took my manservant Jem, but he left with my blessing to take the license on a coaching-house, and it is appropriate that this time we will have Mrs Motcomb's Barnaby. Servants move from place to place at the merest hint of a better, but Barnaby has stayed for twelve years, she says, and has both watched over Tom and is trusted by him; and what he still has to learn as a valet he more than makes up for in matters equine. This means that we will hire vehicles, horses and drivers as we see fit, and are unlikely to be cheated in that regard. We will take local guides where needful but I will act as general courier.

Mr Motcomb will arrange our Letters of Credit, and I must write my advance notices.

Venice is important here, because of the demand for accommodation at the best time of year. That is to say, during the months after Carnival, when the theatres are open, the excitement still ripples but is less dangerous, and the Ceremony of the Espousal is observed, when from his ceremonial barge the Doge casts into the lagoon a wedding ring.

This, amid crowds that are all the greater for the improving weather, that half Europe wants to savour, re-affirms the Republic's marriage to the sea, and to its own unchanging ways.

When the nuptial trumpets blow, I tell my bears, there is a resonance for all Britons: the virtues of our own trade and Constitution.

FRANCESCO CONTARO

I met the mainland lawyer in a coffee-house near Rialto and he was not the old fox I expected but a youngster fresh from his training.

"Signor Contaro? Marvellous. I'm Alfredo Trevisano. Father hopes you'll go easy on me. It's my first difficult mission."

He ordered a scrape of nutmeg on our coffees, and spotted the confectionery.

"Pistachio paste," he said. "Can't resist. Daydream."

Daydream? Is this how the young speak today?

"Why do you think that I can help?" I said. "I am at best an acquaintance of Signor Rovigo."

"Of course. We know that. Where to begin? How much do you know about the testator old Signor Braccio?"

"Lawsuits? Goats? Mulberry leaves?"

"Mulberry leaves. Of course. Holy Mary."

He had a bright little eye, and drew himself up, as though to address the Court.

"The essence of the case is that Signor Braccio purchased his nobility. Four hundred thousand. His inheritance when he was a very young man."

I was surprised. I had thought that Braccio's father bought it.

"A catastrophe. Fifty years ago, but the estate's finances never recovered," said Alfredo, and licked green slime off his finger.

Provincial clumsiness, I thought. The thing is to know how to hold a pastry in the first place.

"When father was appointed he did what he could to effect economies. Such as get rid of the private gondolier."

I did know this because the rower in question was Enzo's father. But I said nothing.

"What would round this off is a gelato. Don't you think?" said Alfredo.

"From the early berries," I said. "It's the time of year."

"One of father's clients ships the snow, you know. Down from the mountains. All that."

"Master Alfredo," I said. "What's wrong? What's happened?"

"Coming to it. In the end old Braccio went ga-ga. No decisions. No Power of Attorney. Bad to worse. Hello," he added, to the waiter who gave him his gelato. "Then he died. Old Braccio, I mean. So who was the heir and – Well –"

"I know about San Marco," I said.

"Of course you must. Well. We found Signor Antonio but what followed?"

"He arrived unannounced?" I queried.

"He did. He caused chaos. Confused everyone. So the Factor sent a man for father, and when father arrived he attempted to explain the situation. Signor Antonio's reaction to this was very unhelpful."

"He has found it hard to trust people," I said.

"Oh, it's not just that. He's locked himself in a room and won't come out."

"Won't come out?"

"He says that he will come out for someone called Rosa."

He gestured with his spoon, scooped the last liquid residue of his gelato, and smiled. Hopefully.

"I do know Rosa," I said.

"Father thought as much. Can we talk to her?"

HENRY ARDEN

Letters written, including one to the Venetian pimp Signor Contaro. I do not like him very much, and he does wear make-up, and scratch himself and wriggle inside his clothes, but he is within his limits indefatigable, and useful to many. I have new stout shoes bought with my advance from Mr Motcomb and in Clerkenwell my books and sundries are packed away in my landlady's attic. She will as usual let my rooms while I am away. I have conversed with Barnaby, an adroit-seeming man with a scar on his brow, whom I surmise to be as stalwart as he is evasive. He knows, I am sure, far more about Tom than anyone has told me. I have warned him that it is when bears have an undeclared confidant on the Tour that they run wild, and he assures me that he understands. We watch each other. Will he divulge more when he is surer of me? Am I equal to this task? I feel twinges in my spirit, as well as in my knees and ankle. In truth, it was my own selfish enjoyment of the Tour, and my vanity of knowing more than the rich persons I escorted, that muddled my attempts to settle down. Again, if Miss Marsden had consented to marry me those twenty years ago, what then? A different life, I think. Tomorrow we sail from Harwich to The Hook.

FRANCESCO CONTARO

We have spoken to young Enzo, whose father has a friend who owns a market boat. This brings produce from the mainland twice a week and can land us at the jetty used by Antonio's own carts. This will be a slower way to reach the Villa than hiring our own boat, but cheaper, and the lawyer will cover the cost.

HENRY ARDEN

Is there no avoiding the egregiousness of McSweeney? There he was at Harwich, grinning in the wind, and leading an Irish lout whom he introduced as Lord Bassett of Bassett Mountbassett. They were to sail after us, for which I thanked God, but today their carriage overtook ours, and McSweeney thrust his arm in a rude gesture from one window, and Bassett of Bassett Mountbassett his entire, ginger-haired, naked arse out of the other.

"Man or woman?" scribbled Tom on his pad.

"Neither," I said. "It was an unspeakable buffoon."

Then I thought: can he in truth be so ignorant of anatomy? Surely not. I decided that he must have tried to be sly with me.

FRANCESCO CONTARO

After the mess of late autumn and the skeletons of winter the plain glittered with spring rain. The mule carts jolted and splashed. On the horizon the mountains were black against fading light. We were shivery. Then the Villa was another silhouette, but with splashes of torchlight. A central bulk, low wings, men in the courtyard, and Antonio. He wore an old ball-gown with a man's goatskin jerkin over it, and a woollen cap like a sailor.

"What? What! You two? Holy Mary! Can't wait to tell you. Amazing discovery!"

"Why aren't you locked in a room?"

"Never mind that. Polenta."

"What?"

"Polenta!"

"Never heard of it."

"Of course you've heard of it," said Rosa.

I was bad tempered. I needed to urinate and get warm but Antonio rushed us through the hot kitchen and rooms which because the logging for fuel had been ignored he could not heat into the estate office and a mess of papers in the lantern's shadow.

"See? Nothing up to date. See? No accounts. Contracts missing. See?"

"Did you say partridge with red wine and thyme?"

"What?"

"On the polenta."

"Yes. Look. Just what I mean. Pages torn out. What?"

"Can you see that I'm writhing or not?"

"Oh darling, if you must piss, piss into that jug."

I hate the mainland. I am never at ease there. I know that the sweet corn that came from the Americas and fed cattle has become polenta, and that the mainland feeds us and keeps Venice solvent, but it is all too much mud and farmyards for me.

Having said that, there were two days of confusion, laughter, unheated rooms, piles of old Braccio's furniture and of his mother's clothes, of looking at silkworms in their racks, and oxen teams, and warmth in the kitchen, where on the third morning Rosa stamped her foot.

"Antonio," she said, "I know you're spinning like a little top, love, but the wonderful fact is that you've found yourself and you don't really need us any more, do you?"

His gabble stopped and he was subdued.

"But you do realise what's happened?" he said.

"Vaguely."

He did his best to clarify. Some of it seemed true, but some fanciful.

"I'm at home here," he said, "but all that I've inherited is debts. If I sell up I'll have nothing again. There's no solution."

We knew that there was one, but did not think it the moment to say so.

HENRY ARDEN

Has any traveller or diarist remarked upon how loudly Dutchmen laugh? The deepness, the booming in the chest, the reverberatory aspect, and the social looseness, the lack of concern for how it may disturb or distract?

"It's the schnapps," says Barnaby. "If you drink schnapps like that you won't hear the noise you make, will you?"

I wonder myself if it is not also a consequence of republican equality.

FRANCESCO CONTARO

"But why did he lock himself in," persisted Mother, "and why did he come out before you arrived?"

"He ran out of food and water."

"How long was he in there?"

"Three days."

"Whatever did he hope to achieve?"

"It's emotional," I said.

"But the solution's as plain as day," said Mother, and as our eyes met she realised the advantage it could bring us, and wished that she had been less open in front of Angelo, who boomed that Antonio was by no means the fool that he cannot help seeming to be.

"Dear Angelo," said Mother, "how prettily you colour the shades of an opinion."

"I encounter him in the Archives," said Angelo, which I knew but tried not to mention, "and he is consumed by his family's deeds in history."

Our flimsiest chair creaked as he leaned in to confide.

"He has told me categorically that the famous Mother Superior's writings are still in the Convent records but embargoed."

"What Mother Superior?" said Mother. "Which convent? Why is she embargoed?"

Before Angelo could explain Rosa burst in, very energetic, and gave me her eyebrows signal: up and down, up and down. It meant that we needed to speak, urgently and in private.

"Something on the cooking fire," I said, which is my code with Mother for police business, and on the stairs up from the courtyard Rosa told me.

"You've not made it up, have you?"

"This? Don't be stupid."

In the Seraglio a boy's client had confided that he was the valet of the French Ambassador, and had been ordered to assassinate the Doge next Wednesday.

"Why next Wednesday?" said Alessandro Perago. "An anniversary? Some Saint's Day?"

Nobody knew, so he sent for an almanac. His legs were bad. When he sat they seized up and when we walked him they hurt. He already knew that the man Rosa saw in The Seraglio was not the French Ambassador's actual valet.

Rosa and I were pleased with ourselves, because San Marco trusted us, and it was a distraction from the risk we knew we had to take. When I am excited in this way I itch more, but in bed that night Rosa scratched me all over and our cuddle was a long one.

HENRY ARDEN

To enter France from the Low Countries one endures luggage searches and delays at two different Customs Zones: such are the financial contrivances to which a monarchy that will not call parliaments is reduced. I made the point to Tom but he did not look up from his book, a trashy so-called modern tale of ghosts and ruins. He has several such, passed down from his mother, and prefers them to more useful fare. Then Barnaby surprised me by his ability to speak French, and in the queue there were other bears and their leaders, and we heard rumours that McSweeney's Bassett of Bassett Mountbassett had in Antwerp been stuck in a broom cupboard with no breeches, the girl he had lured there having run off with them.

FRANCESCO CONTARO

Wednesday arrived. San Marco had realised that the Doge was to pay a private anniversary visit to a church in which his wife's family had a side-chapel. He arrived by water, and patrollers surrounded his party as they crossed the little square.

Rosa was given a dirty old cloak and pretended to beg outside the church.

The supposed assassin stood with a grin all over his face in an opposite doorway. Rosa recognised him and he was seized.

Passers-by, such as they were, had no idea of what had happened.

HENRY ARDEN

A true gentleman would surely, breeches or no breeches, have had the confidence in himself and his position in society to walk out of any broom cupboard, and be damned to who was watching.

FRANCESCO CONTARO

Even sturdy Rosa trembled and sniffled as we walked home after the arrest. Then we came to a bird-seller setting up and I said "Let's buy some finches for Mother."

Rosa managed a whistle at her second attempt and some birds replied at once.

"These," she said. "These two."

I was distracted by a cockatoo.

"No," she said. "They get bored. Pull out their feathers."

"Assassins," I said.

"Assassins!" echoed the bird, and winked.

"He's not for sale," said the birdman. "He knows too many secrets."

We were amused, and it released more than the tensions of the day.

"The Principessa," said Rosa. "You've got to take the risk."

"I know."

"Antonio's our friend."

"I know."

"She can only say no," said Rosa.

Yes, I thought, and then be a lobbyist on her own account.

"Do you want this lot or what?" interrupted the bird seller.

ENZO

Some people in the district laugh at Signor Francesco and round-heels Rosa but I like them and Mum says it's not their fault that they're in crime to make a living, and anyway it's not the sort of crime that hurts people. So Mum says. Anyway is one of her words. What it is, she says, s overcharging foreigners, like your Dad does in the gondola.

FRANCESCO CONTARO

I became a lobbyist through a mathematical mistake that can happen to anyone. I was pleased with myself in those days. I was effective in my small government job and believed that I could carry heavier responsibilities. I became a popular joker among people whom I hoped could elevate me. But one night I drank too much, miscalculated the cards, and lost more money than I could ever repay.

It was suggested to me that the prosecution of even a minor elected official for gambling losses gives the populace a bad impression of our class, and weakens society. This could be avoided if I renounced a public career and served in a more covert capacity.

The Advocate who made the offer was the owner, with his brother, of the casino to which I owed the money, and added that if I touted for them it would be a cloak for my spying.

What surprised me was the ease with which touting led to the variety of services now at my disposal.

Crasser lobbyists accost strangers in the streets and even the churches, but I am above this. I employ tact, and am discreet. Even so (which annoys me) dealers in pictures and antiquities, and fine craftsmen, can be picky when I saunter into their premises, and I have no entrance to the highest noble houses. But the theatres and concerts are a free-for-all, the coffee houses agreeable, and the lounges and supper rooms of the casino already the haunt of people who want to be helped.

So one acquires returning clients, and receives commission from gondoliers, street musicians, tailors, money-lenders and safe brothels and courtesans. It is a percentages living, of course, and seasonal, and gives me the acquaintance in the night-world of persons who in daylight may not acknowledge me.

One such is the Principessa.

"Rosa thinks you should approach her at once," said Mother.

"Rosa hasn't met her."

"Even so ..." said Mother.

HENRY ARDEN

I was correct. It is clear that Tom finds me comical, although I cannot fathom why, and he neither confronts nor argues with me. Then in Paris he giggled at the sheer effrontery of the place, and in Versailles we glimpsed the French King himself, surrounded by grovellers; and Tom seemed to ponder when I compared this arrogant luxury to the impoverishment of the peasants and their agriculture. Think also, I said, about England's improved animal husbandry. His reactions encouraged me, as we journeyed south, to read passages from the "Gallic Wars" in the original landscapes. But does he listen? There is strength in his character, yet he has intermittent control over it, and seems to be himself unaware when he is absent. Can this be altered? Or is it an inevitable consequence of what happened to him?

FRANCESCO CONTARO

"If she is a Principessa," Mother has been known to ask, and Rosa to snigger at it, "who was the Principe?" A question to which there are as many answers as there are lobbyists with whom the Principessa deals but denies any connection. She is German, opines Mother, or perhaps Baltic, has always known everyone, and when foreign royalty visit Venice incognito she makes their arrangements.

Seventy-something years old, hunched and spiky when seated but dignified when she walks, the Principessa wears a very convincing silver wig and less make-up than many Venetian men. Her windows look over the Grand Canal, and blinds in the Roman fashion diffuse the reflections.

She entertained me that afternoon not as a business person, but because she had known, she claimed, both my grandfathers (which was impossible) and she offered me things Greek in memory of our lost Crete: honey-soaked confections, and retsina, that only peasants are supposed to drink.

"Long life darling!" she said. "I like your new coat: about time."

She owed me my percentages from the introductions I had made during the recently-ended Carnival, and always presented them as a settling up after a few hands at cards.

"Is the list in your head, darling? Do the little sums I lost add up?"

It was and they did. I took the money, but made no effort to continue the conversation. Her eyebrows went up.

"Your mother, darling," she said. "What is it that she wants to ask this time? So long since we met. Her eyesight's gone, I hear."

"She wonders," I said, "if you still broker expensive marriages."

"Expensive?"

"Dowries," I said, "to rescue ruined noblemen."

She thought me impertinent, yet looked in a way that I had not seen before, as if she remembered rueful things. Then her smile was jagged and she said "You little scoundrel, Francesco darling. Who is it? Your fat friend?"

How did she know this?

"Everybody hears. Mulberry leaves. Lawyers he can't trust. So is it true that he locked himself in a room?"

"True."

"But he trusts this washerwoman of yours?"

And how did she know this?

"And what worries you, darling? That if something could be arranged you'd miss your cut?"

I shrugged. One of my shrugs. She shrugged back. One of hers. I knew what it meant.

"Good," she said. "Settled. Now remind me. What is the name of that Englishman who has no idea that he's ridiculous?"

"Arden?"

"He never came this year. Is he dead?"

"Next year," I said. "He already wrote."

HENRY ARDEN

Mortification. In a hostelry outside Lyons I was greeted by a familiar ribald voice that said "So there you are, Arden. Do you think that your man Hannibal was Jewish?"

This is the sort of remark that McSweeney makes in his attempts to shatter my buttoned-up complacency, as he puts it, and even as I answered him I knew what he would do next.

He would let his bear cub loose in some prank that would make a fool of mine, and in consequence embarrass me. He had done it before, I explained to Barnaby, and he would have no care for the fact that Tom was afflicted. What should we do?

"What will it be?" said Barnaby. "Cudgels? Cards? Women?"

"They're Irish," I said. "It'll be drink."

"Our Tom's seen more than you think. Trust him."

To my credit, I did. There had to be such a moment. Then he might trust me, in return.

So I was in my nightclothes when McSweeney blustered in without knocking and said "Hiding again, are you? You'd best be outside. You man's spewing his ring up."

Which he was, in the alley, to the laughter and mock-disgust of the kitchen girls. I ignored it, and when Barnaby popped his head in he said "If you think our man's bad you should see theirs."

Then in the morning Tom forestalled me. Upset belly. Must have eaten something, said his gestures, and he made retching and wet shitting noises. He was yellowy-white but fit to continue, while of the others we saw no sign.

We now hear on the road that Bassett of Bassett Mountbassett was incapacitated for four days, and their schedule thrown into confusion.

"Let those who mortify be mortified!" I said, and Barnaby nodded. He is a follower, he tells me, of bare-knuckle pugilism.

Where was he? What had happened? The ship had sunk during the attack, we knew, burned to the waterline, but what of him? Was he dead or alive? He was alive. He was dead. No. The pirates had sold him with the rest of the crew in the Tunis market. Another rumour said Tripoli, and another Algiers.

The Islamic rulers denied all knowledge. The Senate, weighing the cost of the attacks, sent three frigates to bombard Algiers. There were negotiations and new treaties, and some captives were returned, but not my brother.

We were told that he had always been dead, killed when the ship was taken. We wore black, and it was some sort of relief, until we were told no, it was a mistake, it was not him at all.

Father offered a reward and a year later a Greek seaman tried to claim it. He had been in prison with Venetians, he said, and they had told him that when others came home my brother had stayed, of his own accord.

He stayed? Of his own accord? He converted? Could it be believed? What had he suffered to do that? What had he feared? Had we ever known his true nature? Why had he rejected us? What had we done?

Mother combed our memories like a wig for nits, but if unstoppable joy in life is not joy, if every month we bleed to no avail, if mother and sisterhood amount to knowing but not knowing –

We trusted the Doctor. He was Balkan like us and had graduated from Padua, and it was not his fault that Mother lied to him. She accumulated the opiates he prescribed, and killed herself.

Why was love sent to sea with my brother, when this is what happened?

HENRY ARDEN

On a slope of the Vosges I ordered the chaise to stop, and got out. There was a haze over the blue distance and a hum of insects. Our feet grated on the rough mountain road and I explained that we saw the vista as the Roman soldiery must have seen it. The red of their cloaks was an invasive colour, I said, because the shades of the tribemen's fabrics were those of the shrubs and berries.

Tom sat on the coach steps. He seemed interested. I continued. He moved his jaws as if to speak. A horrible noise issued. It was at my use of the word 'Caesar' I thought.

"Write it," I said, but he had checked himself and gestured: no matter.

Then a horse's urine splashed, and the men laughed, and Tom with them. But Caesar? Caesar? What had that name to do with horror?

FRANCESCO CONTARO

Business had fallen off as usual after Carnival and the Ceremony of the Espousal, and Rosa had free time.

"Let's take your Mother to visit her friend," she said.

Everybody was pleased. The friend was another Cretan who had entered a Convent as a lay sister. Now she was old and in the Infirmary. She knew about our finches and said could we bring them for her to hear, which we did, and she sat behind the grille of the Grand Parlour with her walking sticks and a young nun played a cembalo, which set the finches trilling.

Did we realise, boomed Angelo, that this was the very Convent in which the embargoed Mother Superior founded the Choir School?

"Ssh ...!" said everyone, and giggled, and it was one of those afternoons to remember, and not even spoiled when, as in our happiness we shared some light dishes in a supper-room of the casino, I was summoned to San Marco.

There was another wanted man scare, and as I waited a patroller I knew came along the corridor and said: "Heard about the French valet assassin?"

"What?"

"Who he was."

"No."

"Doge's wife's brother's uncle-in-law."

"What?"

"Family secret. He'd been kept locked up."

"Really?"

"Escaped. Over the roof. Done it before. Last time he went to the Arsenal and said he was a Turkish admiral."

"Where is he now?"

"Where d'you think? Locked up again. San Servolo."

Locked up. San Servolo. The island asylum run by monks.

"Is this true?"

"Not all of it."

"But –"

But I was called in for the briefing.

"A Florentine diplomat has been accused of High Treason," said the Advocate. "Tuscany wants him back."

"You mean he's here?"

"False papers. Entered the Republic during Carnival." Carnival. Thousands of people in masks. Anybody could be anybody.

"We think someone's hiding him."

"What sort of someone?"

"That's it. He's always had important friends. High level. So it could be delicate."

"You want me to look?"

"No. To listen."

I understood. A Tuscan accent. Or a servant buying extra because of a guest. But where?

ANA PAVIC

When something is alive it feels pain, and for a long time pain was my existence, until one day I awoke not to sunshine but to a mist that obscured the clutter of shipping in the Basin, and there were only sounds. Splashes. Voices. Bangs of rowlocks. Nothing hurt. I was numb. I thought: I must be dead. Have I grieved? I did not know. Will I? Can I? Should I?

Father had turbulent emotions and said why should we pay Convoy Fees and arrive with all the other ships so that prices are depressed? My brother had agreed. He took the risk, sailed alone, and was attacked.

Now Father mutters like a crone. What's the meaning of this money? Of what use is it? Ships, cargoes, insurance, emeralds paid for in Amsterdam and sent to Goa. My investors. Old nobles who were venturers once but sit now on mainland estates. Jews from the ghetto. Foreigners. The fortunes we made. Will they buy me the return of dead people?

He mutters, and I am an object in his cabinet. No-one knows me because no-one visits us. Balkan friends are weary of our sorrows, and Venetians who need us for business do not regard us as their equals.

Sometimes, I stand outside the cabinet and study myself through the glass. Then I leave myself behind and go into the city.

For two Carnivals now my friend Renata has dressed us in men's breeches and masks, and we have made great mischief.

FRANCESCO CONTARO

Signor Angelo saw Mother to bed and left, and she said "I'm comfortable. You go up to Rosa," and before I did I took her a spoonful of honey and she said "What have you heard? Anything?"

She meant about Antonio, I realised, and we had not. Too

early, I said. It will take time. But inside I was worried. Had we tried to exploit our friendship once too often? Should we have told Antonio? Had he found out and did not want to see us? Too early. Be calm.

But Mother could see that I was not, which I suppose is why I told her about San Marco and the Florentine.

Neither I nor Rosa were sure about this and Mother, whose life now is listening, said "Why hide if you can find a ship? Isn't that what he'd want?"

HENRY ARDEN

Amid boulders women drew water from a pool of snow-grey melt water, and one looked up as we passed. She so resembled Miss Marsden as I remember her that my heart jumped. Yet what an upstart folly it was, to think that she would ever have considered me. I was the wheelwright's son whom her father the Colonel recognised and sent to Oxford for a scholarship, which I won. But it did not make me one of them, even if I inhabit their ideas and think them the only way to be civilised.

I cannot wait now to be in Italy again. It is after all where people find themselves, if they have the courage to look.

ANA PAVIC

Why not? Father is dead of a seizure and I have inherited his fortune: cash, three ships and a palazzo which we had begun to rebuild, filling in the courtyard to make huge floors, but stopped when the piracy happened. I employ a lawyer, clerks, two captains I trust and one I do not, and the domestics.

Father bought the palazzo to show that we were foreigners who beat Venetians at their own mercantile game, and until my brother disappeared believed in our family luck. Has it returned now, in this unexpected way that can make me a Venetian noble? If it has, why not follow?

My lawyer has been approached by three noble families with offers of marriage. They are ruined and want the money I can bring. But so does this Antonio, and his offer came not through men but through women. Why not marry on my own terms? Are women supposed to? No. Not even in Venice. But because I am dead I think I can.

HENRY ARDEN

We entered Italy over the Mont Cenis, four miles up and six miles down in carrying-chairs, the porters drunk and argumentative, the fur rugs they provided very worn. In Turin we met other English, from whom for the most part Tom held himself back. Why would a dumb person undertake the Tour, they wanted to know, and he was not inclined to answer. He immersed himself in my books, across the pages of which, I now discover, he has written strange comments. WHY DO GOSHAWKS TAKE SNUFF, for instance, in a copy of Tacitus.

FRANCESCO CONTARO

When as a noble I attend a Meeting of the Grand Council, it makes me proud to be a part of history, even though we Cretan nobles have no influence and if truth be told pay little attention. At the recent Meeting I dozed off, and was confused because I woke up during the ceremonial reading of the names of those who had embezzled the Republic's money, some of them centuries ago. Who were these men? Had I voted for them? I felt foolish, and went alone to Florian's for a cordial.

A waiter asked me what had happened and I did recall that there had been a report on the rise in shipping profits after the defeat of the Barbary pirates, but no details. I had not listened because I craned for a glimpse of Antonio. But he was not there, we had heard nothing, and it was all I could think about – to the extent that I did not notice across the café a certain Senator.

I had provided his nephew with someone on my homosexual gigolo list, who was an affable lad but stupid, and had argued with the client. This is not what we want, and the Senator came up and demanded his money back.

We settled for half, which was bad enough, and when I told Rosa she said "That's it, you see, love. We should be saving up to buy a lease and have other people do the nasty stuff."

"Saving up?"

"Well, for a start, the money from this Antonio situation."

Situation? What did she know? Nothing, she swore, and Mother said "Of course she knows nothing. She'd have told me."

ANA PAVIC

He is an absurd little person, and insisted on coming at night so that no-one would know. "No flares at the water-gate darling!" said the Principessa, but I did allow light to fall on the steps from the inside. Even then Signor Antonio managed to stumble and get his feet and skirts wet.

"Oh, fuck!" he cried. "I hate gondolas. Shouldn't you tell your mistress I'm here?"

"I am my mistress," I said.

"What?"

"I'm Ana Pavic," I said.

He lifted his sodden hems.

"Wring them out," I said.

He did. He wore a man's heavy shoes, I noticed. Then he saw me in the light.

"Holy Mary!" he said. "St Mark's Bones! You can't marry me, darling. You're beautiful."

"Do you think that you're dressed for this occasion?" I countered.

"Rosa said go as you are, so I have."

There is not a malicious bone in his body, I realised.

"I wouldn't have to sleep with you, would I?" he said.

"Is that your proposal of marriage?"

"Yes. If you like. I suppose it must be."

"Then I accept." I said. "Even if we don't actually marry."

HENRY ARDEN

In a Genoese garden of marble terraces that overlooked the sea, and were planted with cypresses, orange trees and arcaded vines, Tom sat on a fountain basin's edge and made happy noises. We asked why. He could hide there for ever, he wrote, and then did hide, in himself again. In Pisa he emerged for a moment to look at the famous tower and scrawl WHY DON'T THEY JUST NOCK IT DOWN? and in our Florentine lodgings there are more English, this time a moneyed group come to buy antiquities.

They sup late and send out for musicians and are obvious finger-twirlers. That is to say, sodomites. We are civil with them and enjoy their humour but it is clear, thank God, that although they admire Tom's looks, and Barnaby's muscles, Tom himself does not share their inclination.

He has a wry judgement, I realise, of who might mock or hurt him, and who be natural with him. Which, I have to admit, our extravagant gentlemen are.

FRANCESCO CONTARO

I was called to our district police post because the Lord of the Night had been instructed to tell me that the case of the missing Florentine was closed.

"Why?"

The Lord hadn't been told.

"Point taken," I said. "Thank you."

Then self-importance got the better of him.

"Only a rumour," he said. "But Austrian pressure. He sailed to Trieste."

Austrian pressure. Even in our Adriatic the Republic means nothing. Our power is gone.

On the way home I bumped into Enzo, very merry, and with a bundle over his shoulder.

"Enzo," I said. "What's this?"

"Mainland," he said.

"Mainland?"

"Estimates trip."

"Estimates?"

"Big job. Measure up and cost it. Two walls."

Even two walls is a fortune.

"Where?" I said.

"Villa Braccio-Rovigo."

"What?"

"I know," he said, as he set off. "My Dad was old Braccio's gondolier."

HENRY ARDEN

In this vile inn in Radicofani, a hilltop place on the post road from Florence to Rome, and famous in past times for its bandits, a travelling Brandenburger told us that, on the day before, his carriage dog had been eaten by a wolf.

FRANCESCO CONTARO

We had a loud whisper argument on the courtyard staircase.

"You knew, didn't you?" I said.

"Sssh ...!" said Rosa.

"No. I won't sssh, not if –"

"All he did was ask me what he should wear!"

"What?"

"When he went to meet her."

"Her? What her? Why didn't you –"

"Stop shouting! Girls do ask each other about clothes!"

"Antonio's not a girl and I am not –"

"You're the secret police."

"– shouting and –"

"Stop it!" hissed Enzo's mother from below. "Someone might hear you!"

We stopped. Looked at each other. Giggled.

"Two frescoes," I said. "A fortune. On top of what he owes. What's happened?"

ENZO

It wasn't what I'd call a villa, really, not like the ones we saw along the waterway. It was an old farmhouse, but you did walk into this big room two storeys high.

"When you see the housekeeper," said Signor Nero, "she'll be a man dressed as a woman and actually he's the client. So be polite and don't gape at him."

Unbelievable. She, that is he, was fat with a straw hat that had a summer veil and he asked a lot of questions all at once until the Painter's son Signor Gianni said "Signor, let me be the one who worries!" and Signor Nero ordered two farm ladders to be lashed together and sent me up the wall to drop a measuring line. It was scary but I did it.

What they called the horizontals they took from below. Then they made frames of their fingers and looked through them at the walls. Signor Gianni sketched the space and Signor Nero produced his travelling ink-well and wrote everything down in his pocket book.

They asked where we'd sleep, and where we'd have our mixing and equipment rooms, and was it true that a nearby church had just been whitewashed and was the scaffolding for that still stored anywhere, and could it be hired, and they assumed that lime for the slurry could be obtained locally.

What about local men for the mixing and rough labour and, oh, if we needed eggs or casein to add to the paint to make the colours stronger we would expect the farm to provide them.

And all sorts of other questions and as we boated back I plucked up courage and said "What's casein?"

A milky cheese, said Signor Nero, and why didn't I know that?

When I got home I asked Mum. Why didn't I know what casein was? And she said "I don't know. And anyway, it's nothing to do with gondolas."

HENRY ARDEN

In Rome there are tourists of all nationalities, and the bears gossip and give each other ideas; and since the climate is warmer, clothes can become a problem. A carriage shipped from England will have considerable capacity, but when valises must be carried from one vehicle to another, and there is only one servant to supervise, one must plan with care.

It was now clear that despite my advice neither Tom nor his mother had done so, and that he was short of a lighter outfit. I had hoped to postpone such purchases until Venice, where the silks are better and he would anyway need masking gear. But needs must and we took him to a tailor.

There were screens, curtains and watery mirrors, and a boy

brought cups of coffee on a painted tray. When we discussed a second outfit he returned with Vin Santo, and the biscuits as hard as the cutter's eyes. Tom stood in his shirt tails, asked for his pad to write a question, looked vulnerable and was whisked again to the fitting-room. Outside church bells clanged. There were priests everywhere.

Barnaby tapped a bolt of cloth and said "When I was in the navy we ran up our own."

"You were in the navy?"

It would explain much, but before he could reply who should blunder in but McSweeney and Bassett of Bassett Mountbassett, not encountered since the Lyons drinking episode.

They jolted when they saw us, and I fear I was malicious, and struck first.

"A tailor?" I said. "Should it not be a slipper-maker's, for don't you Irish go about barefoot?"

"We'll retire," said McSweeney, "until the place is clear of heretics."

From which I knew him for the secret Jacobite and rebel traitor that he is, and felt most vindicated.

FRANCESCO CONTARO

Rosa always has secrets, to tease and make me jealous, and I often have to tickle her to get at them. Mother cannot see what is happening and one day Rosa made so much noise when my hand was down her front that Mother had to say "Stop! Stop it! You're upsetting the finches!"

"She won't tell me what she knows!"

"Because she doesn't know anything."

"She knew about this Ana what's-her-name."

"Moons ago," said Rosa.

That was it, I suppose. I still worried that something had gone wrong.

Never, said Mother and Rosa; and sure enough, a servant who was Balkan came with a message-tube and inside it a note in Antonio's child-like hand. It asked us to come at such and such a time to an address in Santa Croce.

HENRY ARDEN

We have employed both the plan of Rome by Gianbattista Nolli and the guide by the Richardsons, father and son, to what paintings are on public display. In the Vatican, as we stood before the frescoes by Raphael Sanzio, I read aloud the Richardsons' opinion that whereas the Venetian Titian excites the senses, Raphael improves the mind.

Tom made a farting noise.

"What?"

WOT SAYS WATS BETTER MIND he scribbled.

I discussed: an impulse towards moral good can be equated to a clearer mind. Is such a balance not what Raphael depicts in the fresco?

Tom's gesture could only mean UP YOUR ARSE!

"Don't swear in the Vatican," said Barnaby.

Yet it was after all a discussion of aesthetics, and I was encouraged.

Then in the church of St Peter itself it was impossible not to marvel at the purity of the castrato voices amid the mumbo-jumbo of the Service. But should art, never mind religion, demand such mutilation?

FRANCESCO CONTARO

It was an old warehouse, got up with drapes, armchairs and candelabras, and used as a studio by the pastel painter Renata Penzo; whom we all knew about but had never seen, except once in the casino when she was masked and in a huge cloak. Now here she was at the street door, her apron chalk-smeared, a scarf round her hair, tall, dark, pale-skinned, ironic and red-lipped, at once tremulous and in command.

She winked at Rosa and said "A fine afternoon, Signor Contaro" in Greek, and inclined her head to introduce me to the studio, where a nobleman in the gravest black turned to greet us and with a shock I realised that it was Antonio.

"Oh come on, darlings," he said. "It's only me again. Give us a kiss."

HENRY ARDEN

Was there amusement in Barnaby's eyes as after supper I explained to Tom that it was all very well for him to be vulgar within our circle of three, but that serious discussions with others might be more wisely conducted in moderate terms?

Tom bobbed his head, as if to say true but tedious.

Do I compromise myself by not insisting upon proper idiom at all times? What choice do I have? The Tour is for Tom to make of it what he can, and dumb people have their own notion of the world and its social hypocrisies.

FRANCESCO CONTARO

Rosa's mouth was open. Had we ever seen Antonio in such fine and correct clothing? And Renata Penzo and – there was some sort of a surprise afoot, but what was it?

At the back of the studio a youth's knife banged on a chopping board and Antonio said "Radishes."

"Marvellous," I said, and to smooth the awkwardness pointed at a portrait on an easel and continued "And so is he. Marvellous. Who is he?"

"A Florentine," said Renata. "He never paid me."

"Cheeky bugger," said Rosa.

We laughed and the youth turned and was not a youth at all but as beautiful a woman as I ever saw and my nobleman's calm deserted me and I said "Holy Mary! Ana Rovigo!"

"Not yet," she said. "Maybe never. How did you know?"

ANA PAVIC

How did he know? A memory, he said. Pure chance. Whatever that meant. They are low life, Signor Francesco and his light of love, but irrepressible, and their sorrow at the thought that Antonio might have deceived or laughed at them was so unfeigned that I know them to love him at heart. Plump Rosa came to hug and kiss me.

"Your brother," she said. "I know. Dreadful."

Signor Francesco pranced like an actor and said "Well! What adventures, fair youth!" and Antonio giggled.

"I've told Ana to visit your Mother," he said, "and she can't wait to lay eyes on Angelo!"

Which was true, and we were as merry as old friends are, and kept our secrets to ourselves.

HENRY ARDEN

I know now from Barnaby that in London Tom's visits to the bear-baiting and pugilism were forbidden, because of the sums he lost betting on them. But there must be some exposure to temptation, or how else can we overcome it, and I suspect that the decision to send him on the Tour owed a little to the hope that it might resolve such issues.

So I was on my guard at the arrival of a young Scots nobleman who with his entourage occupies an entire floor of our albergo.

They invited Tom to play dice with them, and he went but would not throw.

"Why not?"

A shrug. A sideways grin.

Later, I asked Barnaby.

"He watched them."

"What d'you mean?" I said.

"Loaded dice. The young lord always wins."

This devious winner is also having his likeness done in oils by the famous Battoni, and Tom was invited to observe a sitting.

RAFFAYEL BETTER he wrote when I asked about it.

We have bought some few small antiquities and curios, but Tom is as interested in pebbles and seashells and bird feathers, and seems to have forgotten that his mother Mrs Motcomb suggested that we arrange a portrait of him by the Venetian pastel painter Renata Penzo.

So long as there's some interest I do not insist. What worries me more is his spelling.

ENZO

Signor Nero read out his calculations. The Painter sighed and said "What other work's on hand?"

Even me and Cormorant knew this. The bedroom ceiling for the old lady, half done, the two Saints on canvas, and Germany.

"Germany," echoed the Painter.

The biggest commission ever. Twice postponed. Difficult haggling still in progress.

"And this Rovigo work would take how long?"

"A hundred and seventeen working days," said Signor Nero.

The Painter and Signor Gianni grinned. Nero's predictions were famous.

"But dressed as his own housekeeper?" he wondered. "Is it

true that he's getting married? Does he know what he wants? Can he afford it?"

The Painter's eyebrows went up.

"Over that time and surface area?" came Nero's answer. "Like I said. Ninety thousand ducats."

FRANCESCO CONTARO

Ana sent for me and asked me to be her Walker. I had to face facts.

"Are you sure?" I said. "I'm not the most reputable."

"I'll give you the money for a cloak," she said. "People won't know that it's you."

This was ridiculous but I agreed. "But anyway," I said, "Why?"

"My visit to your Mother," she said. "Someone has to walk me."

I did, and it was a triumph. We made sure that Angelo would be there and Ana arrived with the ingredients: flour, sugar, salt, butter, eggs and white wine.

"What?" said Mother, both sugar and butter having been sometimes too expensive for us. "You're going to make galani? Oh, Dearest, what bliss!"

Angelo realised who Ana was and displayed his shipping knowledge. She was delighted by him.

"He's so top-heavy," she whispered as we began to cook, "why doesn't he capsize?"

"Ballast," I said. "The weight of his knowledge."

Flour, sugar and salt in the bowl. Add butter. Beat. Add eggs. Continue to beat.

Antonio, I knew, was at the Seraglio with Rosa.

"Now. You pour whilst I keep beating."

I poured the white wine.

Roll it out. Very thin. Cut into rectangles. Score them.

"Antonio rushed into the frescoes," she said, "without telling me. Did you realise?"

"Family history," I said. "Wine galleys to England."

"It was five hundred years ago, for goodness' sake."

"What difference does that make?"

None whatsoever, we both knew.

"Come on. Into the oil."

How they sizzled. What fun she made of everything. Should I have sought such a woman myself? But I have never had a position, whereas Antonio –

Mother's sightless eyes watched me, I realised. This is the wife-to-be of your friend. Be respectful.

We laid the little biscuits out and as we waited for them to cool Ana explained. They would decide about the frescoes and then return to the mainland to oversee the grape harvest.

Then we sugared the biscuits and munched the first ones in silence. They were perfect.

"Could Rosa visit us?" said Ana. "What do you think?"

This was a good example of how fun and joy can hatch problems. Neither Ana nor Antonio know that I am a spy, nor that San Marco wants Rosa in the Seraglio.

I hesitated.

Mother had the answer.

"How kind, Dearest. I'm afraid it's me. I can fumble around in my darkness but I do need a soft hand sometimes."

"Forgive me," said Ana. "Of course you do."

That night, in the truckle at the foot of Mother's bed, I said "Why did she want to know that?"

"Well – if she marries Antonio, she is still free, but she needs help to manage him."

True. Deeply true. But in the silence I thought: and she has great intelligence and realises that there is an anomaly: we receive the state subvention, yet Rosa still works.

Mother sensed that as well and said "Of course ... But what you don't mention she won't, either."

ANA PAVIC

"Why does Rosa work," I said, "if mistresses aren't allowed to?"

"Who cares?" said Antonio. "It's the Seraglio. She loves it. So do I. It's very cuddly. You should see for yourself."

I will, I thought. With Renata. Next Carnival. In our male clothing.

FRANCESCO CONTARO

That same week elections gave our district a new Lord of the Night, a Cretan like most of us: seventeen-year-old Bruno, whom I have known since he was a toddler. This means that we can meet without suspicion; and since it was his first post he sought my advice over the fact that there had been a number of instances of what is in these days an unusual crime – theft from church alms-boxes.

Our own church of San Barnaba had not suffered, but Bruno suspected that the culprit was someone from our district, a man familiar at a distance to us both.

What was also familiar, which Mother and Angelo often recalled, was the fact that just before I was born the city endured the last of its famines and plagues. The population was ravaged and never recovered its numbers. The one beneficial result is that ever since there has been more available work than people, and no need for petty crime.

"So why would he do it?" I said. "Why would anyone?"

Bruno did not know. What worried him was the fact that the traditional punishment had been death by beheading. What did I think, he asked. Would it be the same today?

"You don't decide the verdict," I said. "You investigate the crime and catch the criminal."

"I know, I know," he said.

But I worried for him; and as it transpired, with justification.

ENZO

Cormerant had warned me. "It'll be amazing," he said, and it was. There were wines and sweetmeats and the two Saints on their easels and comfortable chairs brought in and Signor Antonio wanted to burst out with his ideas but the Painter, who knew about the mainland, asked questions about drainage and the rotation of crops and did Signora Ana's family have any old religious pictures and Cormorant kept saying "Wait for it!" out of the side of his mouth and, sure enough, out of nothing the Painter said "So tell me, Signor Antonio. What's your vision?"

Well, it was a gabble, actually, to which Signor Gianni and Signor Nero listened as if they were in church. Signor Francesco looked worried but needn't have, because the Painter held up a very serious hand.

Antonio stopped with his mouth open.

"Thank you," said the Painter. "I could not have put my own thoughts better. A processional …"

Then he reeled off the entire history of the Rovigo family and at the same time drew in red chalk. Slash. Slash. Marvellous. A god with a beard and a big fork in one hand and a shell in the other out of which poured ships, vineyards, forests and – well, just lines, and smudges with his thumb and when he was with us he said very little but now he talked non-stop until he said "Nero, how much would we need as a deposit?" and was silent.

"Ten thousand," said Signor Nero, and gave Signora Ana a one-page summary.

We held our breaths. She read. Then she pointed and said "What's this?"

ANA PAVIC

It was a contingency, said Signor Nero, in case we were unable to provide enough estate carts to fetch the scaffolding. I did not care, of course. The visit was a vivid display to please Antonio, because Nero and I had met and settled everything the previous evening. Signor Francesco I invited because I would need him to Walk me and it was better that he did not feel excluded – and there was the connection, as Nero had explained to me, with the scaffold-boy Boatyard, red-headed and attentive. They liked his intelligence, said Nero.

FRANCESCO CONTARO

Magical. First the boudoir delightfulness of Renata's studio and now this – the Painter's workplace, like those sheds at the Arsenal except that what they made here was not ships but beauty, and that what enchanted us were to them the tools of their trade: draperies and objects, their dogs that appear in every fresco, their books of iconology and history, their knowledge of ancient gods and myths, and of Venice herself.

"Of course," said Mother when I told her afterwards, "and you could have been like Angelo and studied hard and had all that knowledge yourself but for the fact that –"

The fact that I had very little patience and would sooner put down a book and start to shuffle and lay out cards or go out and look at faces and how their little movements betrayed what people felt.

And paying cheap women, of course. Even after Rosa. Cheap women. Feeling handsome when they put a mercenary hand on my arm, and stupid for it afterwards.

"We've had to live in a century of appearances," I said to Mother. "Not much is what it seems, but we can't do anything about it."

And in the studio Ana had nodded at Nero and said "Agreed. When would you start?"

The Painter cleared his throat, and Signor Nero added "If we prevaricate it is because we need to feel that we are free to extend our imagination."

"Holy Mary!" said Antonio, and Ana laughed, full-throated, and the Painter made another red chalk god appear. To my surprise I saw that he looked like me.

HENRY ARDEN

In Naples, which is an absolute and tyrannical monarchy, the contrast between masters and peasants is even more blatant, and the tailoring more vulgarly flamboyant. Tom wanted a striped waistcoat.

"Let him have it," said Barnaby. "When he gets back to Venice he'll realise that it's a daft show-off."

"Lesson learned?"

"Hopefully."

Later, I decided to hide the cost by not hiring a Pompeian guide. I know enough about the place myself to give lectures.

ENZO

A man came from Germany with what they call a draft on one of the banks and a contract for work to start in six months' time. But would my Mum let me go with them?

"Never mind that," said Cormorant, "what about the squeeze on this Rovigo job? A hundred and seventeen days and then off to Germany? No way. And what about the old lady's ceiling? Where's Signor Gianni? What's the Painter doing?"

Nothing. Picking up books and putting them down. Hiring my Dad's gondola and just floating out and sitting there.

But Signor Gianni did come in and do a quick finish on the easel Saints, slapping on paint where his father hadn't completed and we delivered them by water – plus the ceiling which was what they call a roundel in canvas and was waiting for the stucco surround man to finish, which he did, and installing it was another education.

Then one afternoon when the sun was setting the Painter came in with a bowl of shrimps and rice and ate it while we set up shoemaker's globes and in the light of their wicks he did oil sketches of both frescoes in no time at all. Wow!

HENRY ARDEN

At Pompeii Tom was gleeful. He drew with many exclamation marks the volcanic eruptions he had seen. In fact I am sure that he never saw one himself but had talked to persons who did. He is a story-teller, I fear. He told someone in Rome that I was an English government spy.

FRANCESCO CONTARO

The wind that pushes the high water from the Adriatic is a cold one. Mother does not want to go outdoors. I rescued my old heavy cloak from the trunk, but found that it had moth holes; and since my cloak from Ana is more of a display affair, Rosa has given me a gondolier's scarf that someone left behind in the Seraglio. It is rough but effective.

HENRY ARDEN

What to think? Tom reads my prescribed books at last, avidly and even desperately. He struggles with the Latin, asks questions, wants other travellers he meets to describe Pliny and the apocalypse he witnessed. Was it a punishment? Then he asks about voyages, about Jason and Medea and why did she kill her children?

Yet some nights we are easy. We hire the Naples balladeers and their mandolins to sing as we dine outside, in moonlight and still balmy airs, under pergolas of half-dead flowers and discolouring leaves.

FRANCESCO CONTARO

Our extravagance is to buy the gazettes so that Angelo can read them aloud to Mother, and I am surprised, having seen the Painter create a universe before my very eyes, as it were, to realise how many critics attack him. His work is out-of-date, they argue. It is not real, not true to nature like the view painters, or the fashion for scenes at concerts or around card tables. I would like to discuss this with Renata, whose trade is of course portraits of foreign visitors, as mine is to please would-be voluptuaries. So we trade in what market we can. Unfortunately I do not feel able yet to approach Renata uninvited, and Antonio and Ana have returned to the mainland. Their silkworm and cereal harvests were good but autumn came early. Its rain and wind threaten the grapes.

HENRY ARDEN

Unpleasantness. Throughout our journey there have been people who sniggered at Tom behind his back, but few to his face. This afternoon there was, alas, confrontation.

Tom had been calmer. He made not very good sketches of ruins but seemed to enjoy it. He apologised to me for having been excited and indicated that it must have been because he realised that there was history all round him. It could be read up rotten, he scribbled.

Then with Vesuvius in plain view and sunset an eruption of coals upon the water he and Barnaby strolled along the beach.

They were at once run after and jeered at by a mixed group of English and Germans whom we had seen drunk and brothel-bound the night before. Now they cavorted, and imitated cretins, and one pushed Tom over.

He scrambled up and stood back-to-back with Barnaby, the pair of them like prizefighters with their fists up.

They were rushed. Tom's left hand was a ramrod and knocked a tormentor down, and with a wicked feint and blow to the solar plexus Barnaby doubled up another.

At this the pack shouted and gesticulated but withdrew, and against the sun I could not see properly, but for an instant I could have sworn that as Tom and Barnaby held each other at the shoulders they both spoke, very excitedly, but it must have been a trick of the glare.

Anyhow, I have reported our assailants to the English Consul.

ENZO

From the start Signor Nero has helped me three times a week with my letters and numbers, and said I must have Saints, Gods and Virtues at my fingertips, which being Venetian I have a bit already. San Marco with his Lion. Hope with her Anchor. San Sebastian with the Arrows in him. Truth Naked and Unadorned. Great tits, says Cormorant, but not as big as his sister's. Anyway. "Show me more progess," said Signor Nero, "and I'll put you in charge of a sandalo." And he did.

Amazing. Anyway and amazing. Straight down the side canal,

transfer to scows at the junction. Tricky stuff. All the tools my responsibility. Brushes, trowels, floats, buckets, hammers, measuring twine, spatulas, sponges, cloths, maulsticks, lathes, nails, you name it. I saw it stowed and unloaded onto carts at the jetty. Cormorant sailed with the heavier stuff. Signor Nero had his check-lists and Signor Gianni the papers and pigments.

Red Ochre, Haematite, Vermilion, Yellow Ochre, Green Earth, Malachite, Smalt, Azurite, Charcoal. Black, Bone Black, Chalk White. All expensive, and Vermilion worth its weight in gold, says Cormorant.

"All we need is a camel and we're a Timbuctoo caravan," said Signor Nero and Signor Antonio came out in breeches but a woman's shawl. Signora Ana stood by him and there always seems to be space around her. "As though the atmosphere pays tribute," says Signor Nero, and to tell you the truth she is beautiful and I have to feel brave to look her in the eye.

The Painter came next day in a bumpy old carriage. Me and Cormorant have to instruct some estate boys as helpers. They've challenged us to an up the wall pissing contest but Cormorant says we won't get drawn into it until we're sure we can win. We've been given straw mattresses. Very prickly. Anyway. The dogs love it here. They've fucked an estate bitch already. Anyway.

HENRY ARDEN

By what numbers the human population south of Rome is exceeded by bedbugs I do not know, but it must be many millions. Thank God we travel north over mountains and have stopped, stripped, rolled in snow to ease our bites, and shivered naked within our cloaks until the night's inn, where we had our undergarments boiled in vinegar.

FRANCESCO CONTARO

As winter came we saved our candles and brazier fuel and sat in the glow of the kitchen fire and Mother played her box keyboard, that her own Mother had saved from Crete. One night Rosa said "I feel really empty, don't you? Have we done the right thing?"

Mother stopped playing. We looked, but she started again, and next day our pay-off money came from the Principessa. We cheered up, until Mother said "You can't spend it till I'm gone, of course," – and we knew we couldn't, because otherwise Antonio would ask where it came from.

ENZO

With your actual fresco on a wall you start at the top so as there's no damage from drips or your own banging about on the scaffold; and because the top's usually sky, which means clouds and blue, you can do very big day pieces so that people who know nothing about it think that you're working quicker than you are. They see messing about when what we see is planning.

The Braccio-Rovigo walls had the original plaster but the Painter said "It needs another good layer" so we did that first, hacking holes at intervals so that our own layer would stick. While the first wall dried we did the second one.

That was your simple plaster, four parts sand and one part slaked lime to bind, but I soon learned that the plaster for painting was different all the time and depended on what they wanted to paint.

Lime in your plaster lightens your colour, they explained, which is where your eggs and your famous casein come in, because they darken. What they call a glaze is a very thin colour painted over another colour without hiding it.

"Your old timers like Master Veronese used a green underpaint," said Signor Nero as he directed mirrors to reflect light to the very top, under the roof where it's darker, "but we have even more tricks and when they call for something quick up there you know what that means, don't you?"

I did. It meant that I had to be quicker than quick up the ladders to fetch what they wanted. Ceilings could have broad planking, but less light, and for a wall it was better light but narrower planking so they couldn't carry as much up there in the first place, and I remember a call came once for a different brush and when I clattered up with it the Painter said "Boatyard, there's a difference between squirrel and pine-marten fur."

"Sorry," I said, "I'll –"

"Stay there and watch," he said. "I just won't touch it as heavily."

He was brilliant like that. Teaching you without making you feel stupid. Brushes with hair like that they call draggers.

But that was later, to outline hands and clothes. At first it was the sky, the plaster trowelled on and smoothed with a float, the paper cartoon stuck on with nails while the outlines were traced through with a stylus or even a brush handle. Sometimes the tracer pushed too hard and went through the paper; and anyway, when the papers were taken off they were a mess and thrown away.

Then the Painter and Gianni worked on the wet plaster, except that on some of the sky, to make the clouds seem real, they didn't paint at all but let the colour of the dried plaster do the work. When they worked they were no distance from the wall, and at first I thought that what they did looked daft but when you saw it later from the floor – wow!

It was as though you looked through this massive window at a forest and all the gods and people, and I couldn't believe it really, even though I'd seen the oil sketches. Because of course the paper day pieces were distortions to give you the perspective, and anyway he altered things as he went along.

FRANCESCO CONTARO

Christmas came and went and we were in a New Year and then Carnival and foreigners and our money-making time. Sometimes high-class clients would meet the Principessa at a reception, she would give them my name and they would send their servants to meet me in the coffee-house. Then I would arrange what they wanted to happen: the casino, some brothel, a money-lender or an arrangement with a gondolier.

Great courtesans were beyond me, as were those who were more impoverished great ladies than actual courtesans, and grander than the Principessa. It was Mother's great pride that she had never undertaken that remedy.

I trawled on my own account, of course, in theatres and at some of the great sights, and as often as not my nights were in the casino and I emerged at dawn, the violet in the sky and then the red on the water, my eyes prickling, a bad taste in my mouth, and belching. A grappa to straighten my back. Masked people still trailing, the last ashes of torches, lutes still playing in the gondolas. That was when sometimes a lonely reveller would be my last introduction of the night, even though it was day, and if the client was a woman I knew the man for her, and that he would have a reliable Walker to see her home; and if the reveller was that other sort of man I would take him myself to the door of The Seraglio, and then eat a fried oyster or six from the stall outside, and reach home feeling greasy and exhausted.

But Mother would wake me and I would see her to the commode and make coffee, and she wanted to hear the gossip and the alley would echo with noise by the time I went up to Rosa's and slept, sometimes half in my clothes, and hope that I could wake and shave and be spruce for the afternoon coffee-house.

Rosa herself was all night in the Seraglio, where towards the end of Carnival some Germans started a fight and in breaking it up Rosa received a cut lip and a black eye. The owners said "This is a bad look. We'll pay you but stay at home until you're healed," and Mother said "My God, we can't have people thinking you did this, Francesco!" and to Rosa "You'll have to wear a mask all the time."

"I'd sooner have an eye patch," said Rosa.

"Dearest, in a city full of masked people an eye patch is very conspicuous," said Mother, and I said, knowing how much she missed him, "Go to Antonio. Come back when it's cleared."

ENZO

Sometimes we'd work all day and hardly say a word. The Painter and Gianni would nod or grunt, and we'd know what they wanted and it taught you where to put your feet on a plank, I can tell you. Cormorant was the ace mixer, pigments in clean vessels, water, stirred to a paste and Signor Nero checking everything as it was used as well as all the other arrangements, and charming the cooks and stopping Signor Antonio getting slurry on his skirt. I'd climb up with the pigment and there'd be more water pots up there, which you have to be dead careful not to upset. Then they combined the pigments on their palettes and added more water (this was tricky I must say) and it's amazing when they do the faces.

Young flesh is the lime mortar itself with just a glaze over it, and old age has white and grey what they call highlights, and all mouths, eyes and noses done with a very thin brush.

Which is what Gianni was doing one day when I looked down and who should I see looking up but Rosa, and her face was all bashed and I wanted to shout to her but I daren't, although at the end she looked for me and we hugged and hugged and I saw the Painter smile as he rubbed his aches and pains. He's old, actually, and Cormorant says how long can he last?

FRANCESCO CONTARO

As Mother knelt at the confession box Angelo and I waited in the nearest pew. My head ached and I stared at the altar and wondered if I was numb or truly believed. There were revellers in Carnival gear slumped here and there.

"There you are," muttered Angelo, "Regretful of the excesses of the night."

Then there was a bang and a shout and a clatter, and I turned.

The revellers were not revellers but Bruno and his patrollers, and they had seized and forced to the pavings a man who made desperate noises.

I stood. Bruno saw me, and I knew that he had caught his alms thief.

ENZO

"What's this I hear about a pissing contest?" said the Painter.

"We're waiting," said Cormorant.

"What for?"

"Well, Boatyard's still growing, isn't he? When he's a bit bigger I reckon it'll give us the advantage."

The Painter and Signor Nero looked at each other.

Me and Cormorant felt a bit silly, actually.

FRANCESCO CONTARO

San Marco did not care about giving offence to foreigners and yet did care, because the court tried the alms-thief in secret and he was beheaded outside the Ducal Palace at dawn, when stray revellers thought was it real, or was it another street theatre? It was real enough when the blood gushed, said Bruno.

He has been to Paris, and read dangerous modern books about liberty and so-called Reason.

"You must hold your tongue," I said, when we were among those summoned to hear the sentence explained by an Advocate, who said that if we do not maintain our laws, if we do not insist upon what we have always carried out, and upon which the life and stability of our Republic are founded, we are lost, and our identity with us.

As we left the Advocate touched my elbow and said "Might we stroll?"

He wants to know about Bruno and youthful disquiet, I thought, but no –

He was aware, he said, that as a lobbyist I have a supply of English riding-coats, as we call that nation's most useful export, slipped not over the shoulders but on the erect male member, to protect against the pox and forestall conception.

Some eight inches long, and made of rendered sheep gut, they endure repeated use; although some harden and only become malleable again when soaked in water, which can be a conundrum in moments of passion.

Rosa had more than once returned home for dinner, indeed, and exclaimed "Better soak your whatnot while we're eating, love!"

His present emergency, said the Advocate, was that a new maid had thrown his coat away, under the impression that it was a fish skin, although how she could have imagined this when it had a pink drawstring attached he did not know.

The actual explanation, he surmised, was that his wife wanted to get pregnant, when as we know Venetian nobles have for centuries tried to keep families small to preserve their fortunes.

We were on the embankment outside the Ducal Palace and as we arranged delivery and payment the Advocate bought us a gelato from one of the vendors. We looked at the bustle and chatted. His mother-in-law had fallen and broken her elbow, he said.

ENZO

I like Signor Antonio. I mean, I think he's mad but I like him, and I see why Signora Ana likes him. They make each other laugh, and me and Rosa were the witnesses at their wedding in the chapel at the end of the corridor.

The grape harvest had gone better than was feared and we were all given a drink. Nero diluted mine.

Then next morning the Painter said "Everyone outside to study the real dawn!" and as Rosa and Signor Antonio stood with us Signora Ana left for the city. "My honeymoon!" she said to the Painter, and he smiled.

ANA ROVIGO

Signor Francesco walked me from the gondola to the square at the back of the Rialto. "Rosa's fine," I said. "We put snow on her bruises," and he said "I feel honoured. This is a very old custom, isn't it?"

It was. Once almost all merchant business had been done in this square, dealings that reached India and China and Timbuctoo. Today it is an occasional flea-market, but my Jewish purchasers were informed and amusing, and said "Let us meet in the ancient way, at such and such a column in the Loggia."

My lawyer and his clerk awaited and Signor Francesco stood out of earshot. Then the terms were discussed, as in truth they already had been at the lawyer's office.

Then Signor Francesco and the lawyer and I strolled round the square in silence, and the other parties went the opposite way. We re-met at the column, where they conceded my point, shook hands, and the business was done. I had fewer possessions, but a great deal more cash.

FRANCESCO CONTARO

Ana had brought goat cheese and cured meats from the estate, and bread with herbs in it. We helped Mother board the gondola and Enzo's father worked us out into the lagoon, and explained how fishermen from different islands smoked differently shaped pipes, and as we made our floating picnic Ana told Mother that she had sold her ships.

"There's a better return from wine," she said, "and we can improve and build a silk mill."

"A mill?"

"With machinery."

"Machinery?"

"From England. Alessandro Perago already did it."

Did I know that? I couldn't remember. It seemed extra-ordinary.

"Dearest Ana," said Mother, "how long will you stay with us?"

"Until it's all signed and the money in the bank."

"Will you need me to walk you?" I said.

"Could you? How kind. Of course I'll go out the other way, as well."

The other way. Dressed as a man. And that was how the whole astonishment came to happen.

HENRY ARDEN

Haunted by ruins, we wonder if our own world could collapse like that of Rome, and if so, how, and why, and what must we do to prevent it? Again, the ancients are the model for our arts and architecture, but will it always be so? Such are the shadows of our sunny life in Italy. Then we arrive in Venice to be amazed anew. Is it real? On what is it built? Can it indeed be happening before our eyes? What has maintained its thousand years? What is the secret? And the crowds. Armenians in baggy trousers. Jews in their robes. Pastries from their ghetto. Shipping. Yelling spectators at the theatre. The music of this Vivaldi, that is like the ripple of water. The lacquered furniture and the slashed, heaped, beautiful watermelons. Oh, if I could have seen this with some loved woman on my arm!

But I see it now with a difficult boy, and his sorrowful, sturdy and evasive servant.

We arrived at last light, rowed through what would anywhere else be a painting of a fantastic dream. But here actual gondolas drifted, actual lanterns were fireflies that danced again in their reflections, actual music wafted and there was actual light laughter at the water gate of the Albergo of the Heavenly Choir.

This former Palazzo Rovigo, which its penniless owners had to sell, it is the newest establishment to be licensed to accommodate foreigners.

We entered our apartment, and Tom walked spellbound to the balcony and laughed. We joined him. Fireworks technicians were rigging pontoons on the Canal.

Barnaby looked at me and I knew why. What this youth who could not speak expected in Venice was an experience that would teach him about women.

"Not your tumbles and fumbles," as McSweeney once put it in his coarse way, "not your dog and bitch upthrustery, but your –"

Indeed. Your refined sensual commerce become an art that reflects the art of their politics: committees and elections and rotations of offices: power kept alive and not squandered.

McSweeney was at a different albergo, said Barnaby later.

"How do you know?"

He tipped his chin. They'd told him. The servants always tell other servants.

After his enjoyment of the spectacle Tom was uneasy, I could see, and so was I.

FRANCESCO CONTARO

"What is more than remarkable," said Signor Angelo, "is the way in which from generation to generation so much is forgotten, even in our Republic where nothing is forgotten, and more remarkable than that –"

He dipped another piece of bread in oil and chomped on it. A candle hissed.

"– is the way in which although everything changes people do not notice. For example –"

He splashed more drink into his glass.

"– they do not appreciate decline. If things are good for them they think that they are as good as they ever were, even when they are not. What, we may ask –"

Another dip.

"– does this say about their powers of judgement? It is a question that every serious –"

I was beginning to regret that I had asked him my question in the first place.

"– scholar such as myself must attempt to –"

Mother cleared her throat. Angelo hesitated. Then he guided her blind woman's hand to her glass. She drank.

"Thank you," she said. "Dear Angelo."

"What was I saying?" he said, and then "Of course. The Rovigo forests. All cut down now, which reveals a reason, you know, for the decline of our shipping. In Northern Europe wood is not expensive."

"Thank you," I said. "I knew you'd know the answer."

My actual question had been: did the river near Antonio's property have sufficient force to power a silk mill?

"How marvellous," said Mother. "Is all that history what Antonio wants the Painter to celebrate?"

"Four hundred years ago," said Angelo, "the –"

He checked, suppressed a belch, and said "Investment in

earthworks can direct the water to create force. Apologies. I should have said so in the first place."

Then a messenger came from the Albergo of the Heavenly Choir. Doctor Arden and his party had arrived. Could I take them in the morning to the maker of the Carnival masking gear? This did not surprise me. A mask is what all the bears want first, and its rituals explained to them, so that they can feel that they belong.

ENZO

One of the times we held our breaths was when Signor Nero himself mixed a very thin malachite glaze and I carried it up as though it was actual holy blood and the Painter's brush wafted it over the pearls on a woman's collar and they seemed to light up from the inside even though the wetness was on top of them.

At the long supper table I said to Rosa "You should have seen it, and when you get back you will tell Mum that she must let me go to Germany, won't you?"

But she can't leave yet. Her lip's healed but her bruises are still there. They've changed colour again. Actually.

HENRY ARDEN

Signor Contaro was better dressed, for him, but tired, and I suppose that I should have warned him in writing about Tom, but I had not. I lacked the confidence in the subtlety of my Italian and his English. Or so I persuaded myself.

His reaction to the fact that our bear is dumb was effusive but insincere. He embraced Tom and slapped him on the back. "Poverino," he said in Tuscan Italian, and "It is of no importance," in English, and did not look us in the eye.

He went from subject to subject, recommending this

bookseller or that pastry cook, and at the mask-makers surveyed me and said "What about yourself, good Doctor?"

What about me indeed. Is a disguise appropriate for a clergyman? It is not, in my opinion.

Yet the charm is insidious: the tricorne hat, the black settle cape that hangs from it, the white half-mask that can be pushed sideways, the cloak, and the little lantern for night revels – and there was a troupe of improvisers in the square outside the shop, tattered in truth but seeming gay and gaudy, their masks grotesque, their voices like the caws of seabirds.

FRANCESCO CONTARO

This distraction pleased me. It meant that I did not have to speak. Something was wrong. I did not know what, not yet, although I had my suspicion and felt my alarm. When I did speak it was unconvincingly, about this and that, and I thought San Marco's bones, but I wish Rosa was here to whisper common sense.

The boy Tom: good-looking and impatient and he wanted to wear the gear at once, and the servant, Holy Mary but what a presence, like a patroller you trust with your life. His eyes suspected and warned me.

I suggested the coffee-house. We could make our dispositions, there, I said. Thinking: this is bad. This could sink the unsinkable gondola.

HENRY ARDEN

"Not willing to disappoint or disrespect you," I said to Contaro, "I will pay your retainer, but I wish to conduct the business myself, and with the Principessa."

"The Principessa."

"You know her?"

"At a distance."

FRANCESCO CONTARO

And thank Holy Mary, I thought, thank Mother, thank Rosa, thank even Signor Angelo and Enzo's mother and his father the gondolier and –

HENRY ARDEN

"What reason you have, Doctor," he said. "This is not the usual for the money, this is what is for the best spiritually. It will need a very particular woman to induct a boy who cannot speak."

"You know of such?"

"Me? No. But the Principessa …"

What he inferred, I said to Barnaby later, was not so much a woman of the ordinary people as an impoverished noble. A Cretan, wondered Barnaby, one of those who never recovered their position?

I suspected not. To teach life's refinements does after all need someone well-acquainted with them.

In the coffee-house Signor Contaro produced his message tube, a cheap one of steamed and glued wood, I saw, and called for writing materials.

"Your man," he said, "can take this at once to the Principessa."

FRANCESCO CONTARO

"I have also," said Doctor Arden, "written to the portraitist Renata Penzo. We have an appointment. Are you aware of her?"

"Of course," I said. "She talks to me in Greek."

Which was true as far as it went. What is important, after all, is to maintain the Good Appearance.

HENRY ARDEN

I had anticipated a crowded affair, so that Tom could be judged in company, but there were only the three of us and the Principessa cooked herself, little rice and fish dishes over a brazier in her side-closet. She produced cards and said "Teach me an English game, darling," and Tom wrote SNAP IT IS, and it was, and it amused her, and like him she did not cry out as the cards coincided but snapped her fingers.

Then the fireworks went off on the Canal and Tom went to watch and she said "This is not easy, darling, but he has his own looks and a smile, you know, and some say this is enough, so I think I know the person."

"Who?"

"A Signora Barbara. A woman of refinement. Trust me."

They would be together for several days and go out in masks to places where he must treat her with courtesy and learn perforce the gentler side of manhood.

"It is the preparation for life," she concluded. "The University of San Marco, as we say."

I had trusted the Principessa before and I did so now. The actual meeting would be a surprise. We must keep our appointment with the pastel painter, she said, but after that go each evening to a certain canal side at a certain hour and one night a cabined gondola would come and Tom step into another world.

McSweeney once referred to such craft as 'floating double beds'.

136

FRANCESCO CONTARO

They had Anton Maria Zanetti's guidebook to hand and wanted to see paintings by Titian. To compare them with those of Raphael, they said. I knew a private owner of two who for a consideration allowed an inspection.

We stared at a portrait that smouldered with the sitter's intelligence.

"The Principessa," said Arden. "Thank you."

The price would be more than he had earmarked, he added. He would be unable to hire supper musicians.

I could hear Rosa's voice. There you are, love. Bang goes your commission again.

I missed her. For the first time in my life I wanted the season to end.

HENRY ARDEN

Nights at theatres and concerts and rowdy dinners with other bears and their leaders in the Albergo, and then our appointment with the pastel painter. She is a slim woman, and contradictory: awkward but confident, direct but considerate. She offered cakes and thimbles of coffee and arak, which seemed fiery for a woman. But then it is Venice, and Venetian women, they say, are first Venetians and then Christian.

Then out of nothing she asked Tom "How do you see yourself?" and he half-grinned and held up the masking gear.

Renata Penzo nodded. It is what most of the bears want: to be Venetian, the mask itself pushed to the side and their eyes shining. So she accoutred and positioned him and sometimes worked with speed, her tongue at the corner of her mouth, and sometimes walked about and considered the angles, and at others chattered and was amusing.

And there was a youth in the shadows at the back of the studio, but I could not discern him properly.

FRANCESCO CONTARO

In the darkness, on the truckle at the foot of Mother's bed, I could discuss things with myself alone no longer, and confided.

"But I know," said Mother. "You told me. Young Bruno saw his head cut off …"

"I don't want to report anyone ever again," I said. "I'll need to tell lies and seem useless …"

"You did that before," said Mother. "Many times."

Had I? Of course. Don't all spies say what their masters want to hear?

"Go to sleep," she said, knowing that I would tell her eventually.

HENRY ARDEN

On the designated embankment we waited by a wine-stall and then there was a gondolier's cry as his craft swooped near and then checked, swaying, for Tom to step aboard and be swallowed by the curtains; and passers-by had indulgent smiles because they saw what had happened, and my reaction, and knew what it meant.

ANA ROVIGO

Dead people are shameless. They will do anything to return themselves to life. They will cut, burn, bankrupt, disgust and prostitute themselves; yet what they least expect, and perhaps least want because death holds no dilemmas, is the restoring bloodrush itself, the dizziness that overtook me in one spasm, when in Renata's studio my eyes saw his and his mine, and the only reason for the world's existence was for me to speak to him and hold him and for him to hold me and speak to me and whatever had happened before was unimportant.

In the gondola he was not clumsy but gossamer and he laughed and I did not know one word he said to me but –

He loved me on the water and aboard the sandalo and in the window-curtained carriage and words rushed. Mine he did not understand either.

FRANCESCO CONTARO

"Have you told me everything?" said Mother.

"No."

"When did – Ssh!"

Signor Angelo on his way to squeeze lemons. He's in the other room. Safe again.

"Can the boy speak or not?"

"He can," I said. "The boy can speak now."

Signor Angelo swore. There was juice on his lace, it seemed.

"Stand still, sir. Please let me, sir," said our skivvy.

"Where have they gone?" said Mother.

"The mainland."

"But Antonio? What will happen?"

ENZO

She was dressed as a man and he was a girl and then the opposite and Signor Antonio wore a ball gown and heavy boots and gave instructions about digging and planting, and Cormorant, who reckoned he knew about women and sex, said "He wants to come with us on the pissing contest," but Signor Nero said "Not that again!" and to me "What you need to remember is that your Canaletto began with theatre stuff like you, so anything can be achieved!" and Rosa said "San Marco, but it's all gone mad!" and it had, because when people are lovers it's very often comical because they're in one world and everyone else is in another, but this was – well, we were all joyful. We all saw how good and beautiful everything was, even things like goat shit, and one day the Painter took Signor Tomaso up the scaffold and let him lay the light wash over a flying swallow's eye and Signor Tomaso knew words in lots of languages, just words, and I said "What's he saying?"

"I told you," said Cormorant. "The pissing contest."

Liar. And every day was like that. Actually.

HENRY ARDEN

After six days the Principessa said that Signora Barbara, who wished to be anonymous and for no-one to know about her interest in foreign youths, had asked why we were never at the agreed place on the embankment.

"But we were," I said, "and a gondola –"

"What?"

I explained.

"Oh, my God!"

It was not unknown, she said. Notorious strumpets do steal one another's clients in this way.

"He can't speak! He's not safe. He can't –"

The Lord of the Night came to the Albergo at dusk. He was a youth of about Tom's age named Signor Bruno. His patroller was squat and well-armed, and they were unsurprised by what I told them.

But it was not a crime, said Signor Bruno, with politeness, to invite a man to board a gondola, nor to dally with a lady for longer than intended. Mistakes occur. Revellers sometimes embarrass themselves. The authorities have no desire to be tactless. They know of no unidentified bodies or injured persons, and nothing untoward had been reported. So in all probability –

I knew, I said. Tom would appear, with a shamefaced grin, and asking for money.

"Nevertheless, to exhaust the matter …" said Signor Bruno, and asked his questions.

They concerned Tom's safety, and were urgent because of his disability. This made him conspicuous, of course, which was good. But apart from that, how could he identify himself? His papers. Where were they?

For that very reason, I explained, he carried them himself at all times.

"Might he have confided in your servant? Where is your servant?"

Not there. Not in the Albergo. Not there? The first chill.

"Does Signor Motcomb have money?"

"Some."

"Could he draw upon Letters of Credit?"

"No. All such are in my possession."

They looked at each other and Signor Bruno said "Are you sure?"

I went to my valise. The documents had been taken. By which discovery I knew that everything was in ruins.

FRANCESCO CONTARO

"What is it?" said the Advocate. "Is it a scandal among the English? What? Has the manservant murdered him? Where's the body? Should we be worried or prevaricate?"

When we were outside Bruno said "Sorry. But did you tell him everything?"

"Of course," I said. And thought again how easy it is to be a liar.

141

"What was that about the Advocate's mother-in-law's elbow?"

"She broke it. Charming woman. She's on the mend."

And later, in the supper room of the Casino, I pushed up my mask to eat.

My elbow was tapped. A masked woman. The Principessa, I realised.

"What's happened, darling? Is the English Consul involved? Are we being investigated?"

"They asked me questions. I told what I knew. They said fine. Have they spoken to you?"

"But what happened? Who took the boy? Where did he go?"

"They don't know," I said.

"But you must know, darling."

"Why? I'm not that important. Am I?"

"No," she said, disappointed. "No. Sorry. Of course you aren't, darling."

ENZO

When the English servant arrived, the one with the scar over his eyebrow, the Painter said "That's a face!" and sketched him, but what we all felt had changed. Cormorant tapped his nose and jerked his head and said "Trouble. Bad news. Seen it before!" and Signor Nero said "Just mix your pigments!" But he and Signor Gianni did glance at each other and Signor Antonio wore his half-mask and Rosa had her arm round him and said "You've done your best, love. Don't blame yourself. It's for them to decide."

"But I want them to be happy!"

"Of course you do. But you heard what she said."

"Why can't we all live here together?"

He was like a child and even from the scaffold we could see that they were crying, and then Signor Tomaso and his man were in the room, not in masking gear or fun clothes but travelling cloaks, and the Painter said "Help me down."

The Englishmen waited and we lined up, the Painter, Signor Gianni, Signor Nero, the plasterers, Cormorant, me and the local labourers, and Signor Tomaso shook every hand and said something in English and we said our Venetian dialect.

Then they all left, the Englishmen to go up the river to Bolzano, and Rosa and Signora Ana to the city, and Signora Ana was the last and when she kissed me I said "But it's not for ever, is it?"

Because I knew it wasn't. I knew that she'd return after the Espousal because I'd kept up with my reading like Signor Nero told me and I knew about the Gods and Heroes. Signora Ana could have gone with them to Bolzano and wherever but she sacrificed her love. She chose duty, for San Marco and the greater cause.

"That's what happened," I said to Cormorant that night, "that's why she walked so upright." But he already knew, of course. Anyway.

HENRY ARDEN

After more days I was exhausted and people in coffee-houses would point me out: that's the bear leader whose bear disappeared, and I would see them speculate. But they kept their distance, as though I was infectious or offensive, and it was a relief when in Florian's my enemy McSweeney slumped into a chair next to mine and held my hand like a friend.

Bassett of Bassett Mountbassett himself mumbled that he was sorry for my troubles, and watched from the counter as McSweeney sighed and muttered something Catholic in Latin.

"Church Latin," I could not resist saying. "Not exactly the pure thing."

"Too late for that now," he said, "but you can confess to me, which is I'm sure what you sorely need to do."

I tried to protest but could not.

"Your learning's immense," he said, "but your heart hasn't spoken the truth, has it?"

"Hasn't it?" I had a moment of being pleased to flirt, like a girl, but then felt sick.

He looked at me. How ugly he was, and how worried, both for me and for the truth of things.

"Your man," he said. "Will he come back?"

"No."

"Run away, has he?"

"Yes."

"There was always gossip," said McSweeney. "I did always know about the scandal."

So did I. I had always known, and always chosen not to confront it.

"Caesar," said McSweeney.

"Yes."

"A bloody mulatto slave she took to her bed, and him the boy's father, and then she shot him."

"Yes."

"And your man Barnaby – Well. He's a resourceful sort of bugger. I'd have him help me escape."

We were silent. Then McSweeney grimaced.

"Did they truly see a volcano?"

"How like yourself, McSweeney, to ask that question now."

"What I suggest," he said, "since you're rendered incapable, is that I include you in our party and we take the fastest transport we can to London, and that I go with you to speak to his father."

"He's not his father," I said.

"You know what I mean."

I did. And I was finished as a bear leader, he said, but he knew a party in County Wicklow that needed a librarian.

ANA ROVIGO

Antonio loves a bedtime story, and says that sometimes the oldest tales can come true. A dumb person can through the power of love find speech again. He had always known it, he says, because his mother told him, but he never thought that he would live to see it. Thank Holy Mary, he says, thank San Marco and thank Ana Rovigo my dearest wife through whom this miracle was worked.

My lover swore as he licked my ear that I had given him the power, and I am sure that I did give him the courage.

And I think of the mother, by whose son I pray I am with child. Her hot hell of lies in which the boy never spoke and no-one was punished. No-one was in flames or turned to ash. They were in London, flaunting wealth.

What gown should I wear for the Espousal? Your faintest blue watered silk, says Rosa, within which my heartache will proclaim that I'm alive; and the black for the meeting the next day with Alessandro Perago, to discuss English machinery manufacturers.

HENRY ARDEN

Somewhere near Verona McSweeney stopped the carriage and under the season's first blossom we spread a cloth to eat. I was dizzy. Drink never did sit well with me. Bassett of Bassett Mountbassett picked his nose and muttered.

"It's like the decipherment of a corrupt text," said McSweeney, "particularly when his mouth's full."

What Mountbassett seemed to say was that when they were drunk outside Lyons Tom told him everything: and how he'd go to the slave market and buy everybody and set them free, except that he'd no money and didn't dare.

"Well, now he does dare," said McSweeney, "but has he the money?"

"Christ," I said. "Why can't we run away?"

"Because we've no money, neither," said McSweeney, and Mountbassett bit off half a sausage.

FRANCESCO CONTARO

When Rosa came home it was talk talk talk for days on end. All the gossip. All of it. How Antonio had wept for them and – How Enzo was – How Rosa said – How Ana told the Painter that – How Signor Tomaso kept my message tube to Barnaby because it was like Cupid's arrows and – How Signor Nero bowed as they departed and – And then we were ourselves again and it was the day of the Espousal and in our best clothes we took Mother on the water and described everything, so that her blind eyes knew that it was the same as it had always been. The Senators boarded the great gilded barge and it was rowed clear. Then the Doge threw a gold ring overboard, and Venice once more espoused the sea. Enzo's father rowed us as near as he could to the drama. Small boats swarmed, foreigners marvelled, great men wore their robes and fine ladies their silks, none of them as subtle as the sheen of Ana's, as she held the parasol for Mother. Rosa giggled because Signor Angelo dropped a boiled egg in the water and Mother said "Oh dearest!" and then, as the ancient trumpets sounded, she wept. For our Republic, she said, that all the world envies because we have the secret of longevity.

In 1797 General Bonaparte led an army into the Italian provinces of Austria, the enemy of revolutionary France, and went on to seize Venice, that symbol of oligarchic and corrupt aristocratic rule. For two days, to await the arrival of artillery trains, his headquarters were in the requisitioned Villa Braccio-Rovigo. Then he pushed on, and the thousand year Republic collapsed, with neither the means, nor perhaps the will, to save itself. Under the direction of a man named Pietro Edwards many works of art were looted and sent to Paris, but few by the Painter. He was already out of date, his subject matter antiquated and absurd in the ages of change and the modern. Then after two hundred years he was recognised again as the last, the very last, of the Venetian grand masters; and the fresco of the cloud-rocked gondola was cleaned, with funds given by a Silicon Valley billionaire to an American university, which had purchased the Villa to house its Summer Research Seminars. Anyway.

School Trip

BASTARDINO

Before I even started school we'd play in the alley and courtyards and when other kids called me bastard I didn't know what it meant. I thought: is it something I can't see, like warts or a hump back or bad breath? But Mother said, "It's because your father died before you were born." Which I knew anyway. Today I repeat to myself Mother's arguments with my brother (half-brother) but at the time I pretended not to hear, or that it was rockets blasting off, not that there are any space-rockets in Venice. My brother is years older than me and he said, "It's finished here. Who can get work? Venice is finished." Then he went and we never saw him again. Like my pal Raimondo, who's an electrician and went to work in Germany. Just moved from Frankfurt to Berlin, his mother told me last week. Raimondo was the one who explained what a bastard is, and at school he'd defend me. Then after I'd punched a few mouths and made the girls giggle, I didn't care what anybody called me and it became a sort of nickname. I'd grin at it. There were even times in class when I'd be the first to put my hand up and the teacher would say "Bastardino" and I'd answer the question.

I mean, Holy Mary, but what's the difference? I didn't make myself happen, I look good, I'm a good dresser and Maria is seventeen, the age my mother was when she married and had my brother (half-brother) and to hear Maria laugh is magic.

Maria's father owns a shop that sells hand-made paper and notebooks and cardboard boxes to tourists, and he thinks that Maria is too good for a bastard like me. Who am I, he asks, and what, after all, was my Mother?

Well, she worked in the bakery and often we got up before dawn and the baker rowed us in his sandaletto to the uninhabited islands to gather leaves for the herb pies. I'd say, "Can you buy me a parrot for my name day?" and Mother would say "We can't afford it." But it was the leaves, and then eating the pies, and seeing the fish market on the way to the bakery, that got me interested; and Mother saw it and encouraged me, so that often, when Raimondo said, "Football in the yard, come on!" I'd stay inside and cook.

Our food is one of the last glories of San Marco after all, and in school holidays I'd get washer-up jobs and in my last year we heard that the Boss and Signora Boss wanted someone in the restaurant kitchen.

"I've no chance," I said. "They can pick and choose." But Mother said "Go for it," and I did, and they took me on and understood my problem: that I needed to work hard because Mother no longer could.

Her heart. The doctor said "You must be prepared" and I was, but not for how it happened.

One of her pleasures was to cross the Bridge at Rialto and shop in the fish market. I said "Go early if you must," but even early there are tourists taking selfies and no-one buying fish any more, which Signor Boss calls a calamity. After seven hundred years a calamity.

But to obey health regulations even he must buy most of his own fish from the modern wholesalers.

Again and again I said to Mother, "You know what the doctor said. Heat. Crowds. Don't exert yourself. I can buy fish."

"You? You start at seven and finish after midnight."

Her legs were swollen and blotchy and I said again "Promise me …"

Which she did, but broke it the next day, when there was a cruise ship as big as five apartment blocks in the basin and its passengers spewed ashore and half of them wanted to see the famous fish market, so that the Bridge at Rialto was packed and it took a quarter of an hour to cross.

Mother was stuck in the middle of a crowd of Japanese and other people who did not understand what she was saying, but eventually someone did and she was given a seat in a shop but was in pain and collapsed.

Emergency came up the canal in their inflatable but had to

shove and struggle the defibrillator through the people and by the time they reached her she was dead.

That was last year. We cremated her quietly. My brother (half-brother) was told but did not appear.

So I have the two rooms and the shower. Machines outside the pharmacy sell condoms and pregnancy-testing kits. One brand of condoms is called Geisha Balls.

Our restaurant hours are long and not always when Maria can slip away (she is still at school) and we are both nervous and in awe, somehow, which is ridiculous I know in the Twenty-First Century.

So we do not take our clothes off as often as we might.

We did cuddle once last week, when she said, "Your Mother had some cash. Why not buy yourself a parrot?"

"Saving," I said. "Honeymoon."

Then we discussed socks. How colourful should they be? How dignified?

I am angry and crazy and repeat all this because – well, the Advocate did warn me. But I thought months have passed and there is no word and, anyway, who cares what my brother (half-brother) does. But now the worst has happened.

MARJORIE

There is a fake bus-stop in the grounds of the Care Home, where residents who imagine that they have to catch a ferry, or return to the barracks, or pick up the children from sports, sit until one of the mini-buses finds them and returns them to their rooms.

Dad was neat, his scarf tied muffler-wise, as by the millhands and pitmen of his youth. Next to him waited a flabby bald man wearing nothing but underpants, who as I arrived rose and said, "Take my seat."

"Mr Woodward," said Dad, "climbs out through his barred windows."

"I can believe it," I said, and smiled thanks.

"Ciggy?" said Dad.

"Who smuggles them in?"

"Don't ask. Read any good books lately?"

I told him.

"What? Why? Not going there, are you?"

I was. Next day. So I wouldn't be able to come over.

"Don't say you think you'll find love there ..."

He had, of course. He had taken a cycling summer with his university girlfriend, split up with her in Milan, gone on alone and in the Piazza San Marco met Mum and –

"And the rest was history," she said. "History and fucking soap operas."

Which, failing to be a great novelist, he had written for decades. Now his house behind the untidy hedge was let and the money going towards his care.

"Half term school trip. The ones doing History of Art," I explained.

"It's when she's out of sight, though," he said. "The mistakes. The bloody awful men."

He had slipped again. He thought I was Mum, and that they were discussing me.

"Another staff member was meant to go but – " Don't mention the panic over the School Inspection, I thought. It'll wind him up. "So I volunteered."

He sighed. He couldn't get his lighter to fire. I took it from him.

"Too late," said Mr Woodward. "Here's the bus."

COLONEL VON ALTDORF   1849

Sergeant Mauerbach is one of those people who seem stupid but aren't, which makes him invaluable in our line of duty: spying, that is, in the present case upon the Venetian populace and our own occupying soldiery.

"Why, you ask, does an Austrian officer, off-duty and in civilian clothes, enter the Café Florian?"

More than fifty years ago the Republic of San Marco capitulated to Bonaparte. At the Congress of Vienna, after Bonaparte was defeated, the victorious powers gave Venice to our Austria without so much as a permesso or a prego, after which Florian's would neither advertise itself nor print a bill of fare in the German language.

It became the café of Venetian so-called patriots, of literary types, and of deluded liberals.

In consequence the Quadri, on the opposite side of the Piazza San Marco, became our Austrian café and today, after the decades of our rule, the revolutionary uprisings of the year 1848, the Venetian rebellion and our loss, siege and re-taking of the city, the difference between the cafés remains; although Quadri's has the better orchestra, we believe, and is the choice of most of the foreign visitors who have begun to return to the city.

"Does he meet a woman? A whore? One of what's left of their ridiculous nobility?"

It did not seem so.

"The foreign newspapers?"

No need. After the relaxation of the censorship they are everywhere.

"A preference for Florian's ices? An Italian friend of his own age? You'll be telling me next he wears a slouch hat."

The slouch hats of insurrectionary German students having become an emblem across Europe of support for nonsense about liberty.

"He enters alone, Excellency, and sits alone, and asks the waiters who people are."

Since the Pietro Ziani affair I have been doubtful about waiters in the Café Florian.

"They invent what we want to hear," I said.

"Of course, Excellency, but ..."

He was overtaken by a sneeze and apologised. It is damned

cold even here in Danieli's. Outside there is slime on the stones, and mould, and on the high tide the beaks of the gondolas are lifted over the steps, and peer into the lobby.

But what concerned us both was that the officer wore plain clothes: no badges of rank or regiment: we had no idea who he might be.

MARJORIE

Dad is a smartarse, of course, and I understand why Mum left him and why his second wife the actress did the same and doesn't want to know. But I did give up my job at the Wolverhampton Comprehensive and sell up and become Head of English in this snobby little private school in the commuter belt to be near the Care Home because somebody had to. And because I love him and he has always said amazing things.

Such as: the last truly glamourous thing that an ordinary person can do today is to see Venice rise from the sea as the water-taxi approaches.

"Phooey!" Mum had said when I reminded her. "He didn't think that up. It was that friend of his."

"Friend?"

"The one he was jealous of. The one who wrote for the National Theatre..."

How like her to say that, when she knew how excited I was.

VON ALTDORF

Forty years ago, on the day that Father left to re-join his regiment, he woke me before dawn, walked me into the forest that surrounded us, and reminded me to listen. "Always listen, and the forest will tell you what you want to know."

That day we did hear a far clatter of wings as birds were

disturbed by a predator, and the nearer rasp as a bear sharpened his claws. Our huntsman Franz cocked his flintlock, and the bear must have heard and gone away.

A month later, at Aspern, the only battle that Austria won on her own in the long war against France, Father was killed. Mother went to the attic where he kept his nightingales, threw the cloths over their cages, and passed a brush over parchment to induce their voices.

But they never sang for her, nor for me until many years later, when there were only two of them left.

Franz who had the flintlock is my orderly now, grey and deliberate, and after Mauerbach had gone he watched my coffee grow cold and said, "Will your Excellency walk in the forest?"

MARJORIE

To see Venice more or less for free, and since I had only been at the school for two terms to be able to involve myself more, was a no-brainer, I supposed; at the Comprehensive there were never trips like this, where parents stump up three hundred pounds and more for a few days.

But now, having left my flat at dawn I was by midday (water taxis being too expensive) on the vaporetto with Jeff Brown, Head of Art and organiser of the trip, seven boys and four girls, age ranges fourteen to eighteen, and Mrs Wigley, a parent whose daughter Emily needed supervised medication.

All of us staring at Venice on the horizon.

And the kids agog among themselves about the School Inspection and how one of the pupils interviewed had been Megan Mischief as the staff called her – thirteen, spoiled, arrogant, excluded from two State Schools and wanting to leave ours, she insisted, and get into modelling at once.

She told the Inspectors the school was "an impossible hell" and they asked the Head what she might have meant by this and the Head was flustered but – what the kids didn't know – the Inspectors said it wasn't so much this that worried them as our pathway.

By which they meant a demonstrable rise in our standards, and our rating as compared to other schools.

The fakery, Jeff called it, the pretence that everyone's clever and everything better, so that we all mark low at the start of the year and high at the end.

Mrs Wigley had heard, was concerned, and wanted to ask but Jeff said that all he could say at the moment was that, although, thank goodness we didn't have Miss Mischief on the trip, we did have James Parker. Glue sniffing. Etcetera. Keep our eyes on him.

I took James for English Literature and thought him well-intentioned and weak rather than bad, whereas Harry Elwood – Harry Elwood eyed me sexually and the girls eyed him as though he was God's gift, and I discussed him on the plane with Mrs Wigley, who agreed with me.

Now he wore a show-off silk scarf and the girls excited each other at the sight of Venice but I felt little. I already knew what it would be like.

"Maybe the glamour was the taxi," I said aloud, and Jeff said, "What?" so I explained.

"You mean you feel that you've already seen it? Films? Photos? TV? Can't get past them?"

"Maybe."

I'm thirty-three and worry that I'll always be worried. The year before I thought I'd found someone, but it fizzled out.

"Did the people on the Grand Tour know?" I said.

"What they wanted from Venice?"

"Yes."

"Absolutely," said Jeff. That's the conundrum, isn't it?"

BASTARDINO

The Africans who sell fake designer handbags were sharing a joint in the back alley and grinned as I rushed in.

"Hello Geisha Balls!" said Gino the waiter, and Signor Boss said "How is it in Asia? Do machines in Yokohama sell rubbers called Venetian Nights?"

"Assuredly," said Signora Boss, using the fridge doors as a mirror for her lipstick. "It is known for a fact."

"It's not funny!" I yelled, and threw a pan.

Silence after the clatter.

"Bastardino," said Signora Boss, "What? Why are you late? What happened?"

MARJORIE

Jeff preferred a cheapish hotel to hostels because, he said, there would be other students in hostels, and we were here to study art, not other students. So after we collected our keys and dumped our stuff we met outside and he marched us to a sandwich bar, where he addressed the Harry Elwood arrogance problem before it became a problem.

"The Piazza San Marco first to get us orientated and then etcetera and etcetera. And Harry … if you want to go off sketching for an hour you can, so long as I know I can rely on you …"

Hand on shoulder. Old equals.

Harry, who had already made swanky use of his limited Italian, and boasted about what he wanted to see in one of the etceteras, said "I'll stay with you, sir, if that's okay …"

Mrs Wigley overheard, winked at me, and mouthed, "Brilliant."

BASTARDINO

What to say? My father who was not my father had owned our two rooms that a couple of hundred years ago were built over the entrance to a courtyard, and willed them to my mother, with the proviso that on her death they passed to their only son my half-brother. Who now, said the Advocate, wanted me out.

The kitchen was an uproar of comfort, outrage, and suggestions. Gino's cousin is an estate agent, we'll call him. Lodgings. A widow's spare room. Sharing, even. But who with? Clean the crabs. Cleaning crabs soothes the mind. And even Gino's cousin, we knew, could not afford to live in Venice itself. He drove across the bridge every day to sell rooms in Venice to foreigners. This bleeding of the city, said Signor Boss. Where will it end? And every day tourism fills the restaurant at every service. So there's the heartbreak.

MARJORIE

We stared at the famous Café Florian but could not go in because it was too expensive, and I tried to imagine Mum and Dad in Piazza San Marco when they were young, his long hair, her cheap sunglasses, but it was impossible. Today's crowds obscured them. Backpacks bumped me. Trolleyed suitcases rattled.

In the basilica I wanted to ask Jeff about the mosaics but I couldn't see him. I couldn't see anyone I knew. I'm in this impasse, I thought, waiting for Dad to die, Mum not caring, his second wife nowhere to be seen.

Then one of our fourteen-year olds clutched my arm and said, "Are we lost, Miss? It's fun, isn't it?"

What had Jeff said? Meet between the columns at such and such a time.

So we found them and outside the Hotel Danieli Jeff stopped

the straggle, pointed out landmarks and said, "Let's just pop in here while we've time ..."

'Here' was Vivaldi's Church of the Pieta. Jeff spoke about old Venetian charitable and religious institutions and art patronage and asked, "Any follow-up?"

Anita Sayal said, "My father has Vivaldi on the surgery answerphone."

Her father being a dentist.

"Answerphone?"

"People on hold."

"Excellent," said Jeff. "I've got some on my tablet. I can download if you like?"

VON ALTDORF

Outside Vivaldi's church we stood in our greatcoats and listened to the forest. It was a babel: from the stalls that since daybreak had sold hot fish, soup, mulled wine and even cigars, and from storytellers, a puppeteer and people gasping at a juggler.

But no-one fell silent at the sight of our uniforms, or whistled revolutionary airs behind our backs. All we heard was sing-song gossip.

Then I looked, and I saw the chips and holes made by our cannon and musket-balls. I knew the weight of the taxes we imposed to pay for the rebuilding. I saw brown cloaks and hoods and knew that many were wrapped around poverty and sleepers in doorways and on bridges, and families who crowd into one room with no furniture, and eat from the stalls.

And there were sticky pools where eels lay to bleed out before they were weighed, and lady tourists stepped with care.

But there were picturesque sights, like the orange sails of the fishing vessels; and business people who had come to haggle over a wine and a cigar nodded at me without rancour, and some of the poor women smiled.

And I was reminded, by the burn and shock of a grappa that I had bought from a vendor's stone jar, of plum brandy when we were young, once, and gathered round the piano and sang. My wife's eyes had sparkled. Everyone spoke at once and we were happy and danced.

Then the knocker banged and it was the police at the door.

"It's Lent. You aren't allowed to dance, Excellency, even if you are an officer."

Bloody vulgar peasant oaf.

"Sorry, Excellency. It's duty!"

And as a soldier and a guardian of the Empire's soul and purpose I apologised, because it was Lent and we did know the law and were wrong. Which is how it was in those safe years before the Revolutions, and their freedom which is merely chaos.

It is the same here today, the forest rustle told me. Agitation is dead. All people want is peace, and to improve their lives.

Which means that if the officer in Florian's is up to no good it is not with Venetians but with a foreign power, and it is imperative that we identify him.

MARJORIE

With a jolt and a grating roar the vaporetto engine went into reverse and there were squeals and a cry of "Oh my God!" and Jeff called "What's happened?" and someone said "Charlene's dropped her phone into the water!"

"Well, we can't do anything about it now."

"First crisis," said Mrs Wigley.

But I did not care. I did not care about Charlene or her phone, because there was a man, and his eyes were fixed on mine, and mine on his.

ANA ROVIGO   1849

It can be easier to know ancient history than the lives of our parents. Bonaparte himself requisitioned our Villa Braccio-Rovigo when he waited for his artillery train to catch up and Grandmother explained to him the family history in the frescoes. He was a snob, of course, and she had his measure. Or so they say.

When the Republic collapsed my father the only child joined the French administration. He was an idealist, and thought that liberty was the future, but the wars and blockades ravaged our mainland and ruined our manufactories, and then there were the Austrians and their taxes to pay for their own losses, and Father was restless, and travelled.

To England, they say, and even the British West Indies. He certainly met my mother in Amsterdam and came home with her. By then Grandfather had died, Grandmother was old, and Father middle-aged; and to whatever questions he had asked he does not seem to have found answers.

Mother was young. I was born first and six minutes later my twin Antonio, and some minutes after that Mother died.

Father travelled again. There were the bad harvests, when the peasants had to eat grass and died of foul diseases. Grandmother took us to the city and back again and all I remember of her is the luminescence and the accent. Balkan pronunciation, I suppose now.

She was always a redoubtable manager and hired a good overseer in Mario and a tutor who instructed both of us. Eventually Father kept Mario but dismissed the tutor, and bought an Austrian Imperial title with cash that should have been spent on the silk mill.

And there were the quarrels.

Our lives became a muddle, in which the one clarity was Antonio's anger at Father, and Father's at Antonio, because now Antonio was the young idealist (influenced first by the tutor), the patriot who wanted a free and united Italy.

He joined secret societies and was involved in the Pietro Ziani affair. In the end Father reported him to the police and Antonio ran away.

Then Father died. He refused to recognise Antonio, and made me his heir.

Before I could find Antonio the Revolutions broke out and this time it was Austrian troops who commandeered our harvests.

I learned from a priest that Antonio was in the city, and active in its doomed defence. Then the turmoil was over and it was possible to travel, but I decided to wait and oversee the grape harvest, such as it was, and did not come here until a week ago.

I found the top floor of our palazzo smashed by Austrian artillery fire, and Antonio living as best he might among the wreckage. He was in love with a lawyer's daughter named Olivia, and struggling to recover from his wounds.

Alas, he has not. He goes out, to Florian's, and the dances, but not everything has healed and his balance is unreliable. He bumps into people, and drops things.

I have sent to the Dominican Friars on San Servolo. They are trained at Padua, and by most people's reckoning better than the civilian doctors.

MARJORIE

There were many passengers between us and he did not look at me again but spoke to Charlene and Jeff and I wanted to shove aside the intervening people but he got off at the next stop and walked along the embankment and my eyes followed him and I knew that he was kind and amusing and beautiful and had courage and authority and I thought I'm a fool, I'm crazy after the mistakes I've made and the pain and will I ever have a child, what's wrong with me, and Mum's curled lip and Dad's tact that is actually boredom, and my legs were weak and in my very womb I – then he did look back at me, once, and he did nod and –

"Jeff says he'll buy a pay-as-you-go pro tem," said Mrs Wigley.

"What?"

"For Charlene?"

Oh yes. Charlene. They were allowed to use phones to take photos and for communication if the group straggled, but for nothing else outside their hotel rooms.

"Jeff," I said. "Yes. Very good."

Thinking: has this woman realised? And will she keep schtum if she has?

VON ALTDORF

Our office is in a large but low-ceilinged chamber in the former Ducal Palace and is piled with archive files that have nothing to do with us, and with wrapped paintings. These, we surmise, are from former religious houses, some looted by the French but returned after protests, some commandeered by ourselves but never sent away, some bought by art dealers and awaiting collection.

At Mauerbach's suggestion we unwrap a different one each week, enjoy it or not, and have it wrapped again. At present we have a baroque Saint.

As we stared at it I said, "Attire."

"Excellency?"

"Is the richness of his attire not somewhat at odds with his piety?"

"But no slouch hat," said Mauerbach.

"A bare head in the presence of the Deity," I reminded him.

Were we smug about our little analogy? I suppose we were.

That our officer in Florian's wore street clothes not to invite an approach, but because one had already been made, was our conclusion.

A soldier came in, said "Pardon, Excellency," and walked out again.

Our camouflage is that we are a temporary signals unit awaiting both the arrival of new semaphores and the allotment of other offices.

Then the man we had sent for appeared. He would sit every night at one of Florian's outside tables and when the waiter pointed out our officer follow him home.

MARJORIE

Churches, altarpieces, architectural patterns, the cunning simplicity of Jeff's teaching. Wow and wow. My heart beating. The kids' interest a joy – poets wrote that love makes everything seem beautiful and now it did. Are the eighteen-year olds too young for John Donne? I must discuss this with Jeff I thought and knew what his answer would be. That it is the shallowness of what's around us that makes it seem so. I remembered Dad in his whisky prime sneering that no proper actor would cheapen himself by doing a commercial. He must have hated himself, I realised, hated his own work. Oh the pity I felt and the short breath and in my room at last I masturbated and lay there and thought am I a fool am I a fool and if I had not made mistakes how would I know now that this is the man and –

Knocking.

The door.

"Are you ready, Marjorie?"

Mrs Wigley.

"No. Wait. I'm –"

I'm not even showered and I should have packed my brighter lipstick.

Don't be stupid. How can I ever see him again?

"We'll rendezvous downstairs, Marjorie. No pressure."

VON ALTDORF

In that clearing in the forest the Piazza San Marco there was a crowd for the garrison band's early evening concert. Poor, respectable, pickpockets, children running. Greek sailors, Turks in their baggy trousers, well-to-do English who are easy to spot, we like to say, because the women are badly dressed and the men very pleased with themselves.

There was still some clarity in the sky, and the first stars, and lights from the cafes.

Outside Florian's I pretended to have trouble lighting my cigar, so that I could scrutinise.

Not seeing our man I assumed he was inside, and the crowd seemed innocent enough. Women with their hair dressed and plaited in a circle would be Venetian, and the ones wearing bonnets mostly foreign. Families ordering fork suppers would be local bourgeois, and the men whose clothes were excellent but shabby were old nobles, I reckoned.

There was a scurry when a young man who leant on a walking-stick dropped his wine glass, but the waiters were quick to tidy, and he to apologise.

I moved on and was in the Quadri when the concert ended and boots crashed as the band marched away. The café orchestra struck up: a polka: gaiety: groups of our officers and people I knew.

One asked me to join him for supper but I had agreed with Mauerbach to be on stand-by at the Danieli.

MARJORIE

After the last organised activity the kids were allowed out on their own but returned in time to go out together to the restaurant that Jeff had booked from England. They smartened up and girls wore lipstick. "I'm being phoned from school," Jeff

said on the way. "The Inspection. Panic stations. Tell you later."
Then over dinner he orchestrated a discussion.

"You'll now realise, from the reading we did before we came,
and from this afternoon's orientation, that …"

I was in a daze. It was hard to listen, I said nothing.

"… Venice took architectural ideas from the places with whom
it traded in the Middle East, and …"

Will I see him again? Ever? Never? How?

"… Exactly, Bobby. Well observed. And early artistic ideas
came from Byzantium, which …"

How long had I sat there? Did I eat a starter? What was it?

"… so try to imagine. You're a medieval person and you can't
read or write. How do you learn things?"

Television.

Cheers and jeers.

You stupid git.

"… Maybe not as stupid as it sounds. Oral traditions. And yes,
Lucy. Images. Pictures. It was a world of visual culture in which
profound religious and political ideas were …"

His hands. Undressing me. Inflaming. Reassuring. Knowing
without being directed.

Din. Tiled floor. Bang and clatter. Who ordered risi e bisi?

The waiter was called Gino and made the kids laugh.

Emily's spaghetti slithered off her fork again.

Carpaccio. A painter who's very thin. Ha, ha, said Jeff.

"Sorry," I said. "I suddenly don't feel so great. I must …"

And went outside.

VON ALTDORF

When we re-took Venice we commandeered the hotels, threw out
whoever was there, and installed ourselves without paying. This
was not popular; but since we are happy to encourage visitors
and to make Venice a spectacle only, with what is left of its

industrial and maritime power transferred to Trieste, the situation was soon regularised, and I am lucky to retain my suite in the Danieli and its view of the lagoon – on which I closed the shutters and had dinner sent up.

Franz stood at one side with a waiter's napkin over his arm, and we talked about the woods at home, and what the shooting would be.

He reminded me what a good partridge shot my wife had been, when we served in the garrison in Moravia. Then we were silent, because she was dead, now, and there would be no more evenings when she sang to the zither in warmer rooms than this.

Franz changed the plates and brought a small almond tart but I did not want it. Out of nothing I said, "Democracy is defeated, Franz. We bought it off with fake promises."

"So we old hounds can go home soon," he said.

"Soon..."

He removed the tart, returned, and said, "Would it be time for a grappa, perhaps, Excellency?"

It would, I indicated. I preferred the yellow from Ponte del Bassano and he the white with leaves in the bottle, and he knew that I would offer him one.

And it struck me that in the Piazza I had seen what was important but could not work out what it was.

BASTARDINO

There were four block bookings for dinner, all early, and I thought: it is having to cope with this rush that has saved me. Keep calm, they had said. We'll help you. Work. So I worked. Crabs. The removal of the flesh. The mashing. The oil and lemon juice. The replacing of the flesh. Signor Boss telephoned the Advocate and was given an appointment for the next day. I will accompany you, he promised. But I must have gone into the alley for a cigarette forty times, and never smoked one through. No surprise. Lunch service had been hell. Chinese. The entire Army of the Long March, we said. They had come on a bus for the day. Tomorrow they would be in Verona. The balcony of Romeo and Juliet. Holy Mary, said someone.

I had texted Maria eight times and on her way home from school she met me in the alley.

"We can run away," she said. "Who needs them? Tonight."

She loves me! I wanted to cheer. "But they could arrest me for abduction," I said and she laughed and cried and I said, "Tonight we have the English school party who come each year. Signora calls the teacher Milord Jeff."

"Will there be sexy girl students?"

"The English and the Swedes are the ones most up for it, they say."

"You mean I'm not?"

How is it that women can twist everything?

But in the middle of the dinner service Gino said, "Forget the girls. It's the woman teacher."

"Yes but yes!" said Teresa the waitress, "But what sadness. What emotion beneath!"

"Service!" yelled Signor Boss.

"Blonde," continued Gino. "Great body. Great tits. Then guess what."

"What?"

"She ups and leaves before the second plate!"

"Service!" bellowed Signor. "Are your Geisha Balls covering your ears?".

MARJORIE

Did I know that he would be there? Yes. No. Yes and he was because on the vaporetto he had spoken to Charlene and to Jeff. Where do you stay? Where do you eat? I'll dive into the canal and fish for your lost phone and serve it with the antipasti. And Charlene had to smile and Jeff said thanks and –

I gasped with an orgasm as he kissed me.

In a doorway.

His arm around me as we walked. Stop. Kiss again. People at outdoor tables applauded.

This is ridiculous. It can't be true.

At the hotel the receptionist smiled and in the room we swayed as if in a gondola in the sky.

Everything will be happy. We have found what we always wanted.

BASTARDINO

One of the English boys had a sketch pad, they said, and as they left gave Gino a cartoon. "Bravo," said Signor Boss, "your big ugly ears exactly!" and as we sat in the half dark restaurant Signora Boss said "You've all done well!" and gave us a Vin Santo and the girls sang songs their mothers taught them and Signor Boss said "Here we are and Venice is still Venice!" even though we were on our phones and I was exchanging xxx grope u texts with Maria, so that it must have been after two when I walked home and my key would not work.

I twisted it and banged the door.

Then I understood.

They had changed the lock. My own brother (half-brother) had changed the lock and put a pile of stuff in the alley.

Mine. My clothes. Taken and dumped in a box.

I was shouting and someone opened a window and yelled back.

"Shut up you crazy fucker what …?".

MARJORIE

As grey light seeped he held me and I knew that I was beautiful and we laughed and he said was he mad? Was I sure? My responsibilities. Had he compromised me?

Everything will be happy.

Everything?

Everyone.

You can walk across clouds.

I can walk across clouds.

And he can sneak out of here before anyone knows, and actually I don't care if they do know.

I am supposed to leave Venice in two hours.

Leave?

I told you.

He had.

Why? To go where?

But listen –

Kiss him. Kiss him again and kiss him.

Then never see him again?

Listen. No. Plans can be changed. I'll stay. And with your permission I will ask: is it possible to hold you for ever?

BASTARDINO

Drunks. Junkies. Police with torches. They shake you and ask for I.D. Why don't you sleep in the box? Because I told you it's full of my gear you stupid –

Hey. Language. Jabs in the chest. Later the street cleaners and refuse boats.

I'd pissed on the wall and shat over the edge of the bridge. What else was I supposed to do?

VON ALTDORF

Wakening with a headache I plunged my face into cold water, dressed somehow and in the last of the drizzle and early light went to the quay, bought coffee from a stall and told myself to think. Think, think, and retrace every – but I did not need to.

In the Quadri, it came to me, when my acquaintance repeated what he had already said twice about his aunt's problems with the postal system, my bored eye caught in a side-mirror a man's momentary blank desperation, and the sneer when he recovered himself. He was one of our officers, and I remembered his rank and regimental insignia.

BASTARDINO

Neighbours came out early and some thought that I'd got my deserved comeuppance but most were good and Old Oysterface said "Such outrages are the reason for the Communist Party!" and Signora Bigbum said that her mother always knew that my brother (half-brother) was a little rat because he reminded her of my Grandfather who was taken prisoner in the desert in 1942 and sent to England.

He came back to his wife all smiles in 1946 and then a year later who appeared but an Englishwoman (spent all her mother's savings to get here, some said) with a child in her arms and your Grandfather had married her in a registry office in England in 1943 and –

With no money to return, she had to clean floors in hotels, said someone.

Pulled a salesman who took her to Trieste.

That's not the story my Uncle heard, objected another.

"In my opinion you should see the priest," said Old Oysterface, "even if he is the priest."

Which was good advice as far as it went, but they were arguing now about how Italians were marvellous prisoners of war, not like the Nazis, everyone loved the Italians and they were very useful on a day release.

Evidently.

And then what did your rat of a Grandfather do but –

Why didn't I know all this before? Was it any help? No. So I found my suit, which Signor Boss said to wear at the Advocate's, asked Old Oysterface to look after the box, and went to the restaurant.

ANA ROVIGO

Father Bruno examined Antonio, accepted breakfast with us, and reminisced about our Grandfather. "I saw him when he was very old. He wore a gentleman's ankle length coat and a sort of English woman visitor's straw bonnet."

I looked at Antonio but said nothing.

"To better keep off the rain," supposed Father Bruno, "and how like your Grandmother you both are. Except for your blue eyes."

As I walked him to the water gate he said that he would make up the ointments and send them over. For the rest there was the English pharmacy in Campo San Luca.

"Thank you."

I held his hand as he stepped in to the sandaletto. When seated he looked up and said, "I doubt that your brother will improve much, Contessa, but I will pray."

MARJORIE

Jeff's only rule for breakfast was that everyone should be ready to leave by nine. The kids asked if I felt better and I said "I think I must have got a bad vongole," and they said "Wicked eatery though," and were their usual selves, and had no idea that everything had changed.

Jeff, reading an Italian newspaper, said, "My word, this is extraordinary."

"What?"

"This Ziani."

"Ziani?"

"He's a blogger."

One of the boys had heard of him.

"Blogger?" said Mrs Wigley.

"A whistle-blower," said Ted. "Big business. Organised crime. Links between. Especially with regard to Venice."

"He's Venetian?"

"Nobody knows who he is," said the boy.

"Why's he called Ziani?" said someone.

"It's a cover name, dickhead."

"I would thank you, Jeremy, not to use that word," said Jeff, "and to apologise to Emily's mother."

"Er ... sorry ..."

Giggles.

"Accepted, Mrs Wigley?" said Jeff.

"Accepted."

"Then it's shoulder bags at the ready and time to go."

ANA ROVIGO

I returned to Antonio. He was unhappy and stared at a miniature of his Olivia. "I'll send later to the pharmacy," I said. "I'm cold," he replied, "Aren't you?"

"I just spoke to Emilia," I said.

He nodded. I smiled towards the miniature.

"All this time," he said. "She sends letters that are passionate and constant."

That this was not true I had already realised. Olivia was in

Mantua and there were no letters. Either her father had forbidden the relationship or Antonio himself had done something to spoil it.

Emilia appeared with little pots of charcoal to warm our hands.

How much more had Antonio not told me?

He sensed my question. He had a novel and took it up again: an adventure by the American Fenimore Cooper.

All these happenings in the great wide world, I thought, and Venice no longer a part of them.

"I know that you resent what Father did," I said, "and I know that you don't like what I propose. But we are almost ruined, and what I want to do can save us ..."

It exasperated him. "If Grandfather dressed as a woman," he said, "why care about anything?"

I watched him read and waited.

MARJORIE

He texted me MXXXXX which meant five thousand kisses, and since he sent them every five minutes it was twenty thousand by the time we reached the Accademia, and I thought someone must surely realise. They must hear my phone ping, and wonder. But they didn't. I supervised them through crowded alleys and they talked about climate change.

Will Venice be drowned by rising sea levels? Is that what that film 'Death in Venice' was about, Miss?

Good God, I thought. Nobody knows it's a book. And in my head Dad yelled again at Mum because I'd said I wanted to be a teacher. Education's fucked. The curriculum's fucked. Touchy feely liberal crap. It's you that's fucked, she screamed back, and Marjorie that's got integrity. Was that the time she hit him?

No, I explained, it's a book and it's about – until a boy interrupted. He'd read (travel blurb about Harry's Bar, of course, also out of our price range) about Hemingway and Venice. Which I hadn't, but I did a coherent busk, and when I opened my handbag for the Accademia security guard my phone pinged MXXXXX and I thought this time, surely – but no, and we went to look at the Carpaccios.

A very thin painter ha ha ha.

What is the point of this joke?

Tourists did not look at the paintings but stood with their backs to them and took selfies.

Harry Elwood was doing a cartoon of the scene, I noticed.

Jeff spoke, pithy and amusing. He explained how the pictures were scripture lessons that set the stories in the real city. The clothes, I thought. The puffed sleeves. What did it feel like to be in them?

We moved on to Giorgione, which was like meeting people in life, seeing them entire but not knowing their secrets. As Jeff spoke some kids sat, some knelt, some wrote or sketched and –

I couldn't believe it.

"Count." I muttered to Mrs Wigley.

"What?"

"Count."

She did.

"Oh my God."

"Yes."

Jeff had a hand-sized pad. His aide-memoire. Some sketches. I said "There's a problem."

"What?"

Instead of eleven kids there were twelve, and a strange girl hunched next to James Parker.

"Crikey," said Jeff. "She wasn't at the ticket desk …"

"No."

"Has he picked her up inside or …?"

Or was she in here waiting for us?

"Well …" said Jeff, and called "Hello, James. Who's your friend?"

"What?"

Some noticed. Others pretended not to. It was obvious that they all knew about her.

"She needs us," said James. "She needs help."

An attendant made shushing noises.

Giorgione, I thought, was an actual person. He went to the loo and everything.

Jeff said, "Marjorie, will you oversee here while Mrs Wigley and I …?"

Too late. The girl ran, and her feet made no sound.

VON ALTDORF

"What also perturbed me," I said, "is that the man seemed to have some inkling of who I am. Which is not supposed to be known."

"Shouldn't we assume, Excellency," said Mauerbach, "that foreign intelligence services know as many of our identities as we do of theirs?"

We should. But who would have pointed me out? How? Where?

"Do we get ahead of ourselves here?" I said. "Be frank."

"What made you suspect that he knew you? His turning away? A light in his eye? Or were you yourself …"

He shrugged.

I waited.

"Concern can infect us, Excellency, like cholera …"

This was too much. I have looked into people's eyes for thirty years and what I saw in that officer's was criminality.

"We know he's in the artillery," I said. "How soon can you identify him?"

MARJORIE

An attendant stepped in front of the girl, hands raised, palms outward, and a shrug, like a footballer's disclaimer of the foul he has committed. The girl checked, howled once and breathed in gasps. James Parker looked at Jeff to say 'Don't stop me', and put his arm round her. The attendant walked the group away.

The girl carried a clutch bag and her shoes, I saw, evening heels with red soles. She wore a silk dress and a leather jacket.

"What happened?" I said.

No-one wanted to answer.

"Did you meet her last night or this morning?"

Last night, of course. Jeff builds some disobedience into his system and after dinner allows accompanied time in a gelateria or café. Then they go to their rooms and lights out is at eleven. So to mitigate sneaking out he puts sensible people to room with the ones he doesn't trust, and the sensible boy with James Parker was Rufus, a Nigerian (his father's an airline pilot) I take for English Lit.

Rufus saw the value of conciliation and admitted that he, James and two girls had slipped out.

This well-dressed girl had heard them chatter, approached and said "Are you English?"

"Yes."

"I can't go back. Fucking bitch. Fancy a smoke?"

They sat with their legs over the lip of the canal. Gondolas passed. There were lights on the water, distant music, and the moon above the old roofs.

My back and the insides of my thighs ached with lovemaking and I thought what a romance for them, what a memory, glamour is as glamour does, and they would have passed a cigarette back and forth.

"I have to ask you this," I said, and saw that they were afraid it was about James and drugs, "but where did she sleep?"

BASTARDINO

"The removal of the clothes and the dumping in the street were in contravention of my client's instructions," said the Advocate, "and of course we apologise."

But he did not look sorry, and Signor Boss said, "Might I suggest compensation?"

"The error was caused by the bailiff's misinterpretation of the date," said the Advocate. "The locks were supposed to be changed today, after the termination of this conference."

We waited. I wanted to smash his face in. Signor Boss put a hand on my knee and said, "Five thousand Euros, charged to your client."

The Advocate removed his glasses. He had a polishing cloth in a little pouch.

"With interest, of course," said Signor Boss.

"Or," I said, "I could sleep there until he starts his building works."

The intention being to renovate the place and put it on internet renting sites. People make thousands.

"Work is scheduled to commence tomorrow," said the Advocate.

"What's your best?" said Signor Boss.

"Two thousand."

"Three and a half."

"Done."

I wanted to speak but thought better of it.

ANA ROVIGO

By mid-morning the drizzle became a thin sort of snow that did not lie and Antonio still did not want to talk about my plans. At the same time he would not tell me what agitated him. He had put his book down again and his head ached, and his vision was blurred.

When Emilia returned from the pharmacy with the laudanum he snatched it and drank. He became calm and mumbly.

Had he told me about the siege? The valour. The bombardments. The cholera. The people with money who gave it to the desperate Republic and so lost it. The poor people who cried, "Viva San Marco!" to the end and when we were beaten accepted it because they hold Venice in their hearts where it will surely never die and –

But none of it was what he truly needed to tell me, which he did at last, as we lit candles at noon and snow fell thicker.

"There's a man who wants to kill me, dearest, and I can't refuse him ..."

BASTARDINO

Every alley and quay was packed with tourists and Signor Boss said "It'll be quicker by the foot ferry."

There was a queue. People with back packs. People eating out of containers. People with sunburn. A man in a football shirt who was weeping.

"It'll still be quicker," said Signor Boss.

I texted Maria and she texted back PARROT XXX????, so I went online but there were only two for sale in Venice itself and one was a cockatoo and I shouldn't just blow three and a half thousand on a bird. Looking over my shoulder as we stood in the ferry Signor Boss said "Parrots? Are you crazy? Where will you sleep tonight?"

VON ALTDORF

By noon we had the man's name and knew that he was stationed in one of the forts that guard the lagoon. Such defences would of course be of interest to foreign agencies. They would use a courier, a merchant or sea captain or so forth, to collect the information. The person in command of the operation could be anywhere.

MARJORIE

"This," said Jeff, "is the biggest school trip cock-up since Felicity Morton broke her arm in Amsterdam."

"She's called Cassandra," said Mrs Wigley, "and she wants you."

"Me?" I said.

"You."

And I knew why. I was so deep in love that I saw goodness in all things. Cassandra was sullen, sneering and beautiful and her druggy eyes had seen through me. She's dangerous, I thought, but was flattered that my love gave me power.

James Parker held Cassandra's hand and said, "We know it's a big ask, sir, but what else could we do? She's desperate. She's no-one else to trust."

"Devious little bugger," said Jeff behind closed teeth, and loud, "Very correct, James. But we'll take over now, I think. She wants to contact her father, is that right?"

"Can you imagine," said Mrs Wigley, "on these pavements in those shoes?"

BASTARDINO

"Where's the Signora? She what? Gone? Where? What? Who came to the restaurant?"

A Sanitary Inspector. There were eye-witness reports of the Signora softening salt-cod, as was the centuries-old method, by bashing them against the mooring posts in the canal.

"We gave him a vermouth," said Gino.

As we must surely know, the Inspector had said, European Health Regulations –

"Vermouth? Not a proper one?"

"Commercial," said Gino.

"More, even, than the bastards are worth. Not you, Bastardino. For you the artisan distillation."

He had already suggested that I could sleep in the restaurant. Two tables pulled together. On an inflatable mattress. Borrow one from the Africans.

"The bad news is that he paid," said Gino, "so we may be served with papers."

"Holy Mary!" And "Too much! Too much!" to someone adding parsley to the mussel soup.

Comfortable belly, grey moustache, dramatic gestures: Signor Boss.

"So the Signora ran to escape the Inspector?"

"No, no. After your phone call."

"Phone call?"

The one he made from the ferry queue.

MARJORIE

"Since we're just about to reach Canaletto and so forth," said Jeff, "we'll examine the Eighteenth Century as planned, then have our snack lunch as planned and make the phone calls from the café."

Cassandra said something.

"What?"

"Her father owns a fucking Canaletto," said James Parker. "Sorry. A Canaletto."

VON ALTDORF

I was obliged after lunch to attend a briefing at which a Government lawyer sent from Vienna explained to mainland headmasters and police chiefs the current state of the censorship. Has it been abolished by Imperial decree or by an act of the (cosmetic) parliament? Does the one await ratification by the other?

The lawyer's Italian was not perfect and below a certain level the attendees did not speak German. The lawyer seemed startled by the fact that it could snow in Venice, and I was amused to reflect that it was a sort of family muddle: but the Empire is a family, of course, and one of many tongues and races.

There were policemen there whom I knew to have been enthusiastic fighters for the rebellion, but we took them back because we lacked manpower and they came because it was their livelihood.

Which is why we need to know as soon as possible about the finances of our traitorous artillery officer.

MARJORIE

On the vaporetto Cassandra cuddled against me and said "Be my mother" and I said, "I'm too young. I'll be your sister," and she said "Yes, please."

She still carried her thousand-pound shoes. Her tights were torn and one foot had a bruise.

Then she fell into the open-mouthed sleep of a druggie and I rolled up her sleeve and found the razor marks. She snored. She was a mess but beautiful and it was illogical but I thought I need my proper child. I need his child but with him as her father something like this would not happen.

The vaporetto bumped against the pier and woke her. A crowd shuffled off. Another waited to board, back-packs colliding and mobile phones on sticks. Even Jeff sneered at this and said that all they were there for was to make another tick on a list, but I understood them, I realised, and I loved them for their yearning, their ignorance that puzzled them, their desire to find a touchstone.

And I loved what they stared at, the facades, the vegetation in the cracks, the ancient layers beneath water that in my bed last night he had told me the wash of so many ships and buzzing launches was dislodging and eroding so that the city was disintegrating faster than it could be stuck together again.

No-one notices, he had said, and not enough care, and no-one seemed to notice my arm around Cassandra and her uncertain steps.

On the phone someone speaking for her father had said "Her mother and her clothes are at the Danieli" and now we entered that magical cave, and I asked for the name I had been given.

BASTARDINO

Signor Boss can order what's fresh and plan Dishes of the Day and Gino and Teresa can roll them off their tongues but come service time it's like the football results – there's always a shock, and what people order can surprise you.

That day it was the Risotto al Veronese: twelve ordered at once and I was flung on like an extra-time substitute to make more mushroom sauce.

"It's a catastrophe. It can't possibly have the quality."

"Does it matter? Will they notice? They're Germans."

"It's not them! It's our integrity, for God's sake! Where the hell's my wife?"

At which moment the Signora returned, having entered through the restaurant, announced "A full service and everyone out there happy! Bravo!" and clapped her hands to encourage us as though she had never disappeared.

Signor Boss rolled menacing eyes to say "All questions later!", shook his pan over the flames and tipped wisps of liver into the onions.

By the time the Signora had removed her headscarf and smoothed down her dress the thing was done, and he yelled "Service!".

MARJORIE

She rose to meet us, older than she pretended to be, a satiny blouse with a tie, trousers, low boots with a heel, a fake tan, clever nail colour, costume jewellery. At her side a young, slim mixed-race woman, great legs, sneakers, a tight sweater and leather skirt.

Before I could speak the older woman said "Marjorie, isn't it? This is Bunny, Cassandra's mother's hairdresser. She can take Cassandra upstairs."

"My clean clothes . . ." said Cassandra.

"She's anxious about them," I said, "and joining her father."

The older woman sighed.

Cassandra said "I stink. I need a shower," and sat on the floor.

People noticed. They knew her, I realised. Some were annoyed. One waved. A waiter approached. It cost hundreds of pounds a night to stay there, I supposed.

"Come on sugar-puff," said the hairdresser, and hooked Cassandra up by the elbow.

Cassandra clutched me and her mouth against my ear said "Seen it in your eyes, sister, you're fucking someone . . ."

Then she kissed me, waved at the whole glittering room, and the hairdresser led her away.

BASTARDINO

Signor and Signora Boss do not argue in front of the staff (except of course in the heat of a service, which is not arguing so much as releasing emotions so that we can stay calm inside) so that at the moment of afternoon coffees and maybe a gelato Signora came in from the restaurant and with muscles clenched Signor led the way into the alley.

We heard fierce yelling. Then nothing.

Then one of the Africans put his head inside the door and said "Nuclear Bomb. OK? Then Peace Conference."

Nobody spoke. Gino shook his head. We resumed our tasks.

Then Signor Boss opened the door and said "Bastardino. Please join us. This is of extreme importance …"

MARJORIE

I caught up with the party at the Scuola di San Rocco: half-dark, half-light, marble columns, rich woods, pictures that glowed, stone seats built into each wall. Mrs Wigley sat with a group of the kids and I said "Cassandra's father isn't even here. He's in Qatar."

"Jeff's upstairs with the others. I'm very confused by this building. Qatar?"

"In the Persian Gulf. Why are you confused?"

"Who told you he was in Qatar?"

"The celebrant."

"Oh …"

That would be right, said her shrug.

"You mean you know about the celebrant?"

"The kids know. They're on their phones. I can't stop them. I expect that by now everyone inside the M25 knows."

Then the kids themselves asked questions. Was Cassandra okay? Did you see her mother? Why don't they care about her? What's the hotel like?

187

Someone set off.

"Where are you going?"

"Upstairs to tell James."

"Well tell him, and then get on with your note-taking."

Jeff's policy, I thought: to yield a little and control more.

"Actually," said Mrs Wigley, "it makes me wonder what the world's coming to."

She meant the reason for Cassandra's presence in Venice, which was her mother's idea to mark her divorce, and show that there was still respect, with a ritual of parting, and seventy-odd paid-for guests. In the city of eternal romance, as the celebrant had put it.

It will show, she had said to me, that their souls have not been destroyed.

There would be a ceremony in the Carlo Scarpa garden at the Biennale: poems, music, a tribute written and delivered by the celebrant. The divorced couple would hold hands and at the final moment let loose their fingers, turn, and walk separate ways.

Cassandra's mother and the guests to a fleet of gondolas, the ex-husband to an airport water-taxi.

"What was she like?" said Mrs Wigley.

"The celebrant? Silk blouse. You know ..."

Mrs Wigley knew.

"She apologised on Cassandra's behalf," I said, thinking that I could not wait to tell my love about it all. "It's beyond our radar. Tell me what confused you."

"Oh. Er – Well we don't have places like this, do we? What did they do here? What were they like? Did they believe all this religion?"

I wasn't sure. Did they? Had they? I stared at a painting and it didn't seem to be a sermon. It was just a shocking image of a person's grief, a bit like Cassandra when the hairdresser yanked her off the floor.

She had run off in the middle of the opera, the celebrant told me. Nothing new. I imagine you have the same problems with some of your pupils.

"Youth today. They think they can be who or what they want, whereas we're all stuck with ourselves, really, aren't we?"

Outside, on the quay that Canaletto painted, she seemed about to say more; but didn't, made a face that in the sunlight showed her age, squeezed my wrist and said "Thanks a million. Okay?" Then she hurried indoors.

ANA ROVIGO

To explain, he had to tell me the entire story, from the moment he met Olivia until the moment of him telling me, and when he had finished I waited for him to say what he had decided to do, but he waited for me and when I was silent said "Are you angry?"

"Yes. At the sanctimonious world. Aren't you?"

"I'm scared."

He did not know where to look

"At Florian's. Who knew? How many?"

He wasn't sure. Eduardo had been a shield. People thought that it was just a broken glass.

My mouth was dry.

"Help me …"

"Lift your book," I said. "One hand. Hold it out from your shoulder."

He could, but it wavered. Then it fell. He was powerless.

"Do you trust me?"

"Yes," he said.

"Then this is what will happen …"

BASTARDINO

I thought: what? What? I don't believe it. What? I was ashamed for no reason. Don't look at me. I put my face against the wall. Centuries old. Cracked. Peeling. Insects in gaps. Damp. Electricity cables stapled. Going where? The stink of mould. And noise. No cars but noise. Footsteps. Boats. Voices. Shut up. I want to talk to Maria. She's in class. Text. But they make them switch off their phones and don't I want her to be monster in the exams so that she can go to university? I do. Then she'll be old enough and sod her father. Not that I want to. I want to say I can be my own chef and own my own restaurant and make more money than you. That's all Venice is of course. Restaurants and souvenirs for tourists and –

"Bastardino," said Signora Boss, "this is a great earthquake of course, but think of San Francisco."

We stared at her.

"San Francisco?"

"Built up again, but better."

I started to walk, stopped, and went back.

"You knew. Why didn't you tell me. You knew."

"No, no," said Signora Boss.

"No?"

"I discover it today," said Signora.

"What?"

"For years I suspect. Sure. But was it my business? No. So I don't know until today when I ask."

"But I hate the woman," I said. "I hate her."

As soon as I said it I thought no I don't. I think she's a big disapproving lump but I don't –

"Sorry," I said. "Very sorry."

"It's fine," said Signora Boss. "So she's coming to the restaurant. In thirty minutes."

190

VON ALTDORF

Beneath our shared ideal of the Empire as a family, beneath Austria's stainless flag, we must alas play politics. Our enquiries, it seemed, could reveal matters of great danger and urgency, and the Governor would have to be informed.

But to make everything official at this moment? No. We needed the freedom to act and improvise, so as to be seen in the end as the sole heroes.

At the same time we needed protection, and the ability to shift any blame.

I stared from my window at the afternoon weather's slow improvement, and came to a decision. The Governor's ADC von Baumgarten was sure to be a guest at the same musical evening, and a light word would serve us best.

BASTARDINO

Closed between services, floors mopped, tables re-laid and ready but nobody there, the restaurant is different: it makes you respectful, I once said to Maria, like an empty church. There was noise from the kitchen and street, but it did not seem very loud.

We sat on the two sides of a table's corner, and said nothing.

Then I don't know why but I put out my hands and held hers and said "Is this true?"

"Yes."

"You're my sister."

"Yes."

"I mean, half-sister," I said, and she half sobbed and half laughed, and when she comes from behind her shyness (but why is a forty-year-old woman shy?) she has bright eyes and a smile. Her hair is fading to grey and she'd put on a black dress, and a cameo that I remembered. I'd seen it on her mother and the sight of it brought other memories.

I'd always known, I thought, always known that there was something between Mum and the baker.

Episodes. Moments that I'd interrupted.

"Sorry," she said. "I hoped you'd be told years ago but then Dad died and Mum said 'No.' You look like him, like Dad. Do you realise?"

I did. I managed a grin. Her eyes widened with tears.

"Don't do that," I said. "Julia, love. Don't do that."

"I'm stopping you," she said. "You've got your work. What should you be doing?"

"Sauces. He's been teaching me the sauces."

She snuffled and nodded. She still ran the bakery. She'd had a fiancé, I remembered, who went away to work and never came back.

"It's an earthquake," she said. "Shall we stop for today?"

"San Francisco."

"Did she say that to you too?"

Sod it, but we did laugh. Our first laugh together, as I said to Signor Boss when he came in, found me alone, and sat with me.

He nodded, was silent, and after a moment offered me a try on his vaper.

MARJORIE

Is there any better fun in the world than the conspiracy of a secret love, I thought, as our crocodile chattered its way through alleys and over unexpected bridges from San Rocco to the Carmine, where there were leers at the nudes in the frescoes and, I suspect, comparisons with what some of the kids had sexted, and Jeff said "Before I forget, look at the floor ..."

It was by Antonio Gaspari, he said, a mosaic of polychrome marble, star motifs within frames, perspective tricks like Op Art, and although the frescoes themselves were devout they were like lying in bed with my lover, and I thought I know you're up to no good, James Parker, because I'm up to it as well, and I can't wait.

At one moment I went wet and thought "My God! My God!"

Jeff wanted to know about Cassandra and I said "Should I have left her like that?" but he said "You took her to her mother. What else could you have done?"

"She's a self-harmer."

"We've got them in school," he said. "And social media nasties. You did your best. We've got our own lot to look after."

What a mess, I thought. Dad's a mess. I can't trust him not to hurt me without meaning to, and Cassandra's mother bought her shoes that cost a thousand pounds, but didn't care when she went missing – and I understood how that happened.

Schoolteachers see many parents indulge their children, and as many give up on them. I had given up on pupils myself, just gone through the motions with ones who didn't want to learn, or thought it didn't matter, or wouldn't get them anywhere, or was less important than shuffling their ear-piece music; and sniggered because I was a stupid old cow.

I will talk to him about this. I will be in his arms and we will promise ourselves to do better.

Because I had whispered "Are you married?"

He wore a beautiful old signet ring.

"Do you live in Venice?"

"Later."

"You'll live here later?"

I will explain later.

He was meant to leave Venice that morning, he had said. But he would not. He would stay. For us. To be together as long as we could.

"Miss, what's the Italian for flashcards?"

"What?"

They wrote flashcards to help their research, and someone had run out.

We bought something that would do and stopped at a café. I had a slice of almond cake. Mrs Wigley watched the kids spread their notebooks and city maps and said "I'm amazed at how much I don't know, really."

"When we see this we're all amazed," said Jeff, and I asked him: "Places where great things happen. Do people know at the time?"

"What's more interesting," he said, "is why great things stop happening, and why people don't realise they have …'

Dad, I thought, the half realising and the blaming, and through the heat haze of my awoken self I saw in that noisy café how to forgive him.

"… which is why I've come to think," continued Jeff, "that application aside, what we teach isn't the thing, so much as …"

"What we show them but don't tell," I said.

"Yes."

So the afternoon became evening and the kids' free hour. I showered and lay on my bed and was happy.

Then in the lobby I realised from the girls' chatter that they had been into clothes shops and tried on a lot but bought nothing. They were excited and argued and in the confusion nobody noticed that I slipped the keycard into his hand so that when I returned to my room he would be there.

Jeff did say, as we walked to the pizzeria, "Unusual bloke you exchanged a word with. Any idea who he was?"

No. Another guest?

"Something about him. Didn't you feel it?"

Forever, I could say. All over and inside me.

Over the pizzas two girls had a spat but refused to say what it was about. Mrs Wigley swapped seats with one of them and Jeff gave one of his talks, about how Venice had contained many artisan industries, and the Arsenale's galleys were built on the world's first production line, centuries before Henry Ford's Model T.

VON ALTDORF

Head tilted, and his monacle held at some distance from his eye, von Baumgarten scrutinised the chandelier.

"One has to admit," he said, "that the Venetians were masters in their day."

I agreed, even if to my taste the result was over-effusive: candles set in coloured glass flowers on a writhing mass of glass leaves and branches, all a-gleam and a-flicker.

At least removing our cloaks had not been a penance: there was a stove in the room and the sweetness of burning essences, gilt plasterwork, mirrors, paintings, all a hundred years old in a palazzo built hundreds of years before that, and rented now by a Belgian banker.

And the usual crowd: ourselves, English, French, Russian, German, everywhere in Europe, and a few Venetians. Many of their old nobles are ruined, unfortunately, and some do not want to mix. Their lawyers and entrepreneurs do, of course, and even the Jewish moneymen. A sign of new times. But then money goes anywhere.

"I hear that some of the English," said von Baumgarten, "have installed grates and coal fires." Then in a sideways voice "Who's that?"

"Where?"

At musical evenings the men stand and the women sit in front on rows of chairs, and he must mean that one, I thought: young, dark, superb profile, sadness and her shawl around her.

"Not sure," I said. "But Venetian. That young fellow looks like her walker."

"Which is good, though," said von Baumgarten. "More Venetians here than usual. It shows that they accept us. Life can proceed."

"In reference to which," I said. "I may need your discretion."

He looked.

I told him.

The singers came in, and fussed over their scores and positions.

Von Baumgarten patted my sleeve and re-joined his party.

Perfect, I thought. We are well prepared.

ANA ROVIGO

After dark Venice is silent and noises carry: wavelets, a gondolier's call, the clank of Austrian scabbards on the stones. Eduardo had walked me to the soiree and we muttered about the people.

"Von Baumgarten?" he said.

"The Governor's adjutant."

"Where's the Governor?"

"In bed. A head cold."

"Who told you that?"

"Everybody."

"I can't have been listening," he said.

We both knew why. But I could not have refused the invitation. Our host the banker was my lifeline.

We would still have to make excuses, and leave early to wake early. Eduardo had his repeater watch, that would chime.

VON ALTDORF

If I am truthful I do not like Italian music. Its emotions are too much displayed. And at dances the Italian women never keep good time. But is it not a country of ambiguities? The woman von Baumgarten spotted, for example, was the little Contessa Rovigo, whose brother fought against us during the siege and about whose family many stories are told – there is a concealed illegitimacy, it is said, but I do not myself believe it. Von Baumgarten inclined to agree with me. The whole place is a myth, he said, which it invented to befuddle its own subjects and everyone else.

MARJORIE

Cassandra had been so drugged up, it was winkled out of people, that she had not slept with James Parker but been taken in by two of the girls, so that the blame, and for the younger ones the glamour, was spread. Jeff had to take some sort of action, and banned anyone from going out again after the pizzeria.

"It's not the sort of thing we want your families to know about, is it?" he said, a politic blackmail that shut the grumblers up.

They nickname him Trainspotter for his grin and his woolly hat. But he knows Art College heads and last year got a girl into an auction-house Fine Art course, a trick he'd pulled before; and his phone advice to the Head was to ask the Inspectors to recommend an approach to the Test Marks dilemma. "They made the bed," he says, "so let them lie on it." He's more worried himself that someone like Harry Elwood could cheapen an obvious talent, and he thinks ahead.

After the pizzeria, for example, he allowed longer in the gelato bar, so that there was little time to fill before the kids went to their rooms.

"If you do the rounds of the girls, Marjorie, and I do the boys, I think that covers it."

My body wanted hands and kisses but some of the girls wanted to talk and I did, thinking does the heat in me show and this is shaming but delicious and I could not stop a giggle so that a fourteen-year-old said "Miss?"

"I've just remembered," I said. "I saw a three-legged cat on a scow."

Had I? Was I lying? No, it was when I – I rushed to the next room. Other lights were already out. The girls had torches, of course, and read under the bedclothes as though it was home, and not a hotel.

Then I was free and alone in the corridor that creaked a bit. I breathed deeply and tapped on my door the agreed signal.

Nothing happened. I tapped again. Nothing. He's asleep. I did not want to knock in case people heard.

I checked his texts and called the number. Nothing happened. There was no ring inside the room.

I went down to reception. Jeff was in the bar area with what looked like a large whisky. He never drank alcohol when with the kids.

"All right?" he said.

I signalled yes.

"Scusi," I said. "My keycard. Left in the room."

The night man was slim and North African.

"Of course," he said and we went upstairs.

At the door he said "You want me to check the room?"

"I'll be fine," I said.

He bowed and inserted his pass card. Click. Green light.

"Thank you," I said, and went in.

There was a light on in the bathroom, but nobody there.

BASTARDINO

Old Oysterface had said that I could sleep in his armchair and I did, my feet on a stool, not comfortable; but there were no cold stones, annoying spout drips, insects, smells of mortar and decay, and there was no fear. There was a smell of cat piss, although I never saw the cat, and Old Oysterface did snore and shout to himself in the next room.

"Chewing gum! I need chewing gum!" he yelled once.

I wasn't sure what I needed. Somehow I couldn't believe I was me.

Tomorrow I'd be at Julia's, above the bakery.

She'd needed the time, she said, to clear out the back room. I'll pay rent, I'd said. We'll talk about that later, she said.

MARJORIE

I went to the door. Turned back. Keycard? It was on the bed. My temples hammered. There was pain in my throat.

Go down. Ask. Did by any chance a gentleman –?

Jeff was there. I couldn't.

This was all a secret. I couldn't show it now.

I could not and must not show that, while in charge of other people's children, I'd fucked a man in my room, and then been dumped.

ANA ROVIGO

Eduardo's repeater woke him and he came to rouse me. Antonio had been agitated and said that he would sit up all night, but he had been in pain, drunk laudanum and fallen asleep. We did not wake him. Eduardo's man was at the water gate and the dark became grey as we slid from side canal to side canal, out into the lagoon, and to the chosen low-tide island.

I was calm. What would be would be. If I did not return the banker would still honour our agreement, and Antonio would have money.

There were fishing boats in the mist but they seemed to ignore us.

Then we arrived and saw that the other party had already landed. This was good, because the cold would have entered them more than us.

I wore a man's slouch hat, a full cloak, trousers tucked into boots.

There was mud and moss underfoot. I had the rower walk with us. They queried it.

"Clothes," said Eduardo.

They accepted it. They were in their uniforms, and he was an arrogant little sod, I saw, even for one of them. I was astonished that they did not scrutinise me, then realised that it was because they were agitated.

The one who explained the conditions had a dry throat, and kept having to clear it.

The rower took my hat and cloak and I took the pistol.

We stood back to back in shirtsleeves, walked ten paces each, and turned.

"You have twenty seconds," said his friend, "after the …"

Cough. Cough.

"… after the fall of my arm."

I shook my head. My hair dropped. The arm fell.

He realised that I was not the brother he hated, but the twin sister, and did not know what to do.

I did, of course, and fired.

MARJORIE

Did I sleep? Twenty times. And every time I woke I beat the bed with my fist and spoke aloud. I repeated what he had said and replied why? Why had he never answered when I asked him about his past or where he lived? Where did he work and was there a family and why had he not asked me the same and had I cared or wanted him to?

Not really. Where was the need? He already knew about me.

The rest was for later, he said, when we meet in safe England and live our slow life. This now is for love.

You do not need to worry now, he said. All you need is to allow me to love you.

And he did. I know he did. I know.

Should I call the police? Did he go to hospital? Would they know at reception? Should I –

I woke up weeping. Had I wept myself awake?

Had I phoned? Ten times. Ten unending buzzings. Had I texted? Ten times. Rejected.

Had he bought a phone card merely to text me? Why? Who would do this? Had he thrown the card away?

Shower. Mirror. A retch. Disgust. What had happened to me? Had I splayed myself open and been left like roadkill?

Make-up. Too much. Wipe it off. But I have to be seen by people, so that I know I can endure it – and another day and night of this school trip.

VON ALTDORF

I was in my shirt-tails, and Franz holding my breeches for me to step into, when someone knocked.

"The coffee, Excellency."

"Have them leave it."

I inserted my right leg. He pulled up.

Knocking.

For God's sake …

Left leg. Hand on his shoulder. Pull up.

Knocking.

"Yes!" I yelled.

Louder.

I sucked in my stomach. Franz buttoned the fly.

A voice at the door.

"Mauerbach? So early?"

It was.

"What the hell are you –?"

MARJORIE

Should I pretend to be ill again and stay in the hotel? Has there been a mix-up? Will he appear? Has he doubted but now trusts his feelings? All said aloud on the stairs. Then I stopped and said don't be stupid. He just used you. It's happened before. Just get through the duties of the day.

No. This precise thing has not happened before and I need some sort of defence. I told Mrs Wigley that my period had come early and I might be a bit erratic, and I suppose that she confided it to Jeff, because they paid me the kindness not of solicitation, but of ignoring me most of the time.

So I went where they went and saw what they saw and heard not their discussions but my screeching at myself and did not know which voice to believe. He used me. He was the person I was destined to meet.

Destined? In front of frescoes I can't remember. Text. Rejected. Destined? What am I talking about? There is this sky, these stones, this water and none of it cares about any of us. High love is an illusion of lust.

No it isn't. No it isn't. No it isn't.

VON ALTDORF

Mauerbach's explanation amazed me. Even so. "In order," I said, and returned to don my boots and tunic. Breakfast arrived and Franz served. I ate a pastry, wiped my fingers on the napkin and said "Now. In sequence. What happened?"

"Harbour police, Excellency. The body of an officer was brought ashore by two colleagues, and a handcart summoned to take him to the mortuary."

"His name?"

"A Lieutenant Kollbach. Infantry."

"Known to us?"

"No."

"How had he died?"

"A shooting incident. They were in butts on the lagoon, hoping for duck. He accidentally discharged his piece."

I looked at Franz. We had both seen it happen more than once.

"But you doubted this explanation."

"I saw their boat, Excellency. They weren't carrying fowling pieces."

I poured more coffee.

"And then …"

"And then, Excellency, whilst on the quay, I was approached by one of my sources."

Aha, I would have thought in a jollier moment. Apart from common whores Imperial officers did not often become intimate with Venetian women because we did not trust them to understand our code. It was different for our lower ranks, and Mauerbach made the most of it.

"A source. Can you say who?"

"A youth of the poorer classes, Excellency. A fisher boy. Very sweet."

Sweet? Mauerbach's homosexual? He could be. He could be anything. Oh God, I thought.

"They were on the lagoon at dawn, Excellency. They saw what happened."

Witnesses. We were at the threshold of a scandal.

"As I said, Excellency, Kollbach was killed in a duel."

ANA ROVIGO

I sat in the tin bath and Emilia poured warm water over me and the soap from the wax of our own honey bees was a balm. Then she rinsed me and as I stood up to be wrapped in towels Antonio limped in (there never was much modesty between us) and said "My God. You didn't kill him, did you?"

"I did," I said, and thought: and it means that you can win back your Olivia.

VON ALTDORF

We approached the matter with the logic that has always served us well. Who had brought Kollbach's body to land? A boatman whom it would take time to identify, a brother officer named Kovacs (Hungarian, we presumed) and the military Doctor. The doctor would be the weak link, we agreed, and by midday we had viewed Kollbach's body in the mortuary (the ball had gone clean through his heart and made a huge hole at the back) and traced the Doctor to the palazzo in which he was billeted.

He sat in the first floor saloon with a friend, and they were drinking.

The friend realised why we had come and stood aside. It was a gloomy room, cheaply furnished, and overlooked the side canal. The palazzo was one of these that had been split up centuries ago, and since then housed all sorts. We had passed washerwomen in the courtyard: maybe the shirts were the Doctor's.

"Doctor," I said, "I'd take a glass if you offered me one."

"Thank you," he said.

It was a rough plum brandy. I toasted the friend. He grinned. Broad cheekbones. Slavic. Many of them enlist.

"Duelling," I said, "was so far as I know made legal again in Venice in 1739, and is not forbidden by our Military Code …"

"Thank you," he said again, and nodded several times.

His cheeks were very hollow. Perhaps he had lost his back teeth.

"Mantua," he said. "This girl. Young. Respectable. Father a lawyer who didn't like Kollbach, but Kollbach was …"

He drained his glass. He poured again but spilled some over the stained, tufted cloth.

"Kollbach was mad for her. We said rein back, didn't we?"

Glancing at the friend who said "Rein back. My God. Yes."

"… but the father was … and one day, not sure how, Kollbach found the girl with this …"

"Other lover," said the friend.

"Other lover, who turned out to be – what's his name?"

"Rovigo."

"Count Antonio?" I said.

"Yes."

Yes. Holy Mary, on my mother's grave, and by San Marco, as they say. I thought about it.

Mauerbach leaned in, a bit heavy and sad, and said "And what happened then, Doctor?"

"Well. Rovigo ran off and a week later …"

"The uprising," said the friend.

"We were in action. Then posted here. Then …"

"Kollbach couldn't rein in," said the friend. "Went after him."

"After who? Rovigo?"

"Looked for him. Asked who was who in the café."

Mauerbach did not look at me. I drank. Rough indeed. Probably distilled on the friend's family farm and brought with him, much as I had brought my linnet in its cage.

"And Kollbach found him?" I prompted.

"Two nights ago."

"Not in Florian's?" Mauerbach managed.

"Florian's. Bit of a scuffle. Rovigo's glass smashed but nobody noticed."

Wrong. I had noticed, but misinterpreted. Which I could not reveal, because officers of my repute do not make such mistakes.

"Rovigo's half-crippled, of course. How could he – But he did."

"Challenge."

"Yes."

"And Kollbach accepted."

"We did try to stop him," said the friend.

A duel between an officer and a civilian was a grey area in the

Military Code, illegal under Civil Law, and in our political situation in Venice a nightmare.

Out of the silence the Doctor made an unhappy man's attempt at dignity.

"As a matter of honour, I don't feel it right to say more at the moment …"

He swallowed a burp, and added "Excellency …"

BASTARDINO

Gino had volunteered to come early and help carry my gear to the apartment above the bakery. Julia made us coffee and said "We need a gift for Signora Boss."

"What can we afford," I said, "that has the value of what she has given us?"

"Orchids," said Gino, ever the psychotic (do I mean psychiatric?) smart-arse. No. Psychologist.

And he knew the place, of course, where the florist said "These are the classics, you know, from the Siamese rain forest."

"Don't be theatrical," said Gino, "they're grown under plastic on the mainland."

"Brought there," responded the florist, "by intrepid plant collectors."

He was another of Gino's cousins, Teresa told me later. The entire family is preposterous.

As we entered the kitchen Gino cried "Tarantara!" and hummed a chorus by Verdi. The plant was protected by cellophane and a gold ribbon tied in a bow.

"What happened?" said Signor Boss. "You win the lottery?"

"Yes," I said. "Life's lottery. With your kindness, and that of the Signora."

VON ALTDORF

It was snow-showery again and we were crushed in cloak, greatcoat and boots under the cabin roof of the gondola. The oarsman gave his sing-song call and we swayed round the corner into the Grand Canal itself.

"And where the hell," I said, "was our man in Florian's when after a scuffle this duel was arranged?"

Which was some sort of deflection of my fury at myself.

"I can only guess, Excellency, that he went off sick."

"Off sick?"

Snow blew in on us. We did not mention the man in the Quadri, who we had identified as a Captain Berg.

"Did you know he was off sick?"

"He misled me."

"Pietro bloody Ziani again!" I said.

I closed my eyes. This is the deep problem, I thought. Even we who are in command tell ourselves not what we know but what we want to hear and be heard. It's a miracle the Empire holds together.

I opened my eyes. We went under the Bridge at Rialto.

I said "Mauerbach: how old are you?"

"Er – thirty. I think. I was raised by my grandmothers, Excellency."

"So you don't remember the times of absolute certainty?"

It seemed he did not. His family would have been poor, I remembered.

We said nothing. Soon, the gondola bucked as we came to more open water by the Custom House. Coastal shipping was gathered.

Like it or not, we both knew, we must discuss what the fisher lad claimed he saw and we had dismissed as a mistake, but now realised was true: that Kollbach was killed by a woman.

ANA ROVIGO

In half fading, half metallic light and flurries I went alone, in the poor woman's cloak and hood I wear when I do not want to be looked at, and sat beneath the Dome of the Ascension. The basilica's organists were at practice. Visitors come to hear them, but there were few. There were candles and the dim sheen of the mosaics.

Someone went into a confessional but I had no urge to follow. Foreigners are sentimental about the city, but to me what I had done was to live up to the secret of its survival, if only for one family.

The sale of the palazzo was agreed. The Belgian and his consortium could make their hotel, and I would invest the money in the silk mill and the estate. What I must decide now was how to communicate with Olivia, and it came to me to send Emilia to find Olivia's maid, and do it that way.

If Olivia loves him, I thought, and is what he says she is, she will be damned to Mantua and scandal and come to Antonio. Her father will forgive her when she becomes a Contessa.

And if that's done I'll need a home and husband for myself, I thought. I smiled. I shut my eyes. The music throbbed. What bliss, to let go of some of my resolve. Yet what more I still needed, because despite my cloak I was shivery, at the shock of what I had risked for my twin, and the dangers we still faced.

BASTARDINO

What I needed to do, I realised, while chopping onions, having more or less told Maria about Julia, was to tell Julia about Maria and get them to meet. I mean, I couldn't smuggle a girlfriend into my sister's (half-sister's) house for furious fucking that she's not supposed to know about. Could I? No I couldn't. Did I need advice? Who could I trust to listen while I spoke my thoughts?

It made me happy to realise that the person I wanted to trust was Julia: dumpy warm Julia who runs what's left of the bakery.

Well. It is on a street between two famous churches so there's always a stream of tourists and they sell them ciabattas in the morning and goodies in the afternoon, and people walk along and wipe their fingers on their tee shirts or their shorts.

I wish Mum was here. I just wish she could see what's happened.

MARJORIE

Pain that cannot be stopped is inflamed by what we are forced to be, and who we are with, and mine was rubbed by the school, the kids and where I was. I walked, stared, answered questions ("What do you do for a cracked nail, Miss?") and did not understand their slang. Rinsed? Bare peak? They were shrill at each other.

"Stop it. We're in a public place. What are they saying?"

"Beefin, Miss."

"Beefin?"

"She's not G!" called someone.

G. Gangsta. Hoodies. G is civilised? Their shrugs.

Had they caught me out? Smelled a wound? When was the last time that someone I taught regarded a set book as anything more than a chore? In their grammarless world (the death of art, Dad calls it, he would), they text all the time and hide it from us and don't care if they know anything or not, because they don't believe that our old knowledge will get them what they want.

A degree might, for some: but the degree itself, not the knowledge it implies.

Global warming haunts them but they drop plastic everywhere, and their parents complain when we say that they aren't learning well or quickly enough; and when it suits them take them out of school for holidays. Some, I guess, take coke and complain about knife crime.

"Celia says she hates Venice, Miss. Doesn't see the point of it."

"Is that what they're beefin about?"

"Yes, Miss."

Or maybe texts about body fat or someone being a snake, as they say, or who'd want to see him/her naked? Who would want to see me?

At the Comprehensive it had been ice cream vans at the gate selling drugs and defeated families, not many jobs out there and who would drift into opioids? Here it was unsatisfied money. Did I even want to live up to old fashioned Jeff? Did I still want to be a teacher? I couldn't make my own life work. So how could I help theirs?

BASTARDINO

My thoughts raced: from past to present: how to tell Julia about Maria: times when Mum had said there was nothing when I knew that there was something: when she felt wanted again and – I froze. I gasped. Everyone stared. "The earthquake," I heard Signora Boss say. "The aftershock. This is normal, you know."

I had stopped chopping – "Thank God," said Signor Boss. "We do not want fingers in the risotto." – because thinking about Mum had led me to the Baker.

Am I like him? I have his nose and jaw, I think. But was he a shit, or a man who tried to do his best?

VON ALTDORF

In our office we stared at the painting of the Saint. He looked more serene than we felt. We had received a hand-delivered note from von Baumgarten, saying that in the matter of Lieutenant

Kollbach he would welcome our thoughts, and another from the commanding officer of Captain Berg, the man I had seen in the Café Quadri.

Captain Berg, it said, was in a distressed state because he had learned that his wife in Graz had died in childbirth. He had been given compassionate leave of absence.

"Your Excellency's infallible eye ..." said Mauerbach.

"Yes."

"You recognised a man at an extremity."

And a smashed glass, and waiters kneeling to clear the fragments.

The confusions that we are expected to unravel.

People in ordinary life escape such complexities.

Eventually I said "Honking geese ..."

"Excellency?"

"The forest. We may not see them, but they pass overhead ..."

Mauerbach looked.

My late wife's second cousin had dined with me last week. A diplomat, he carried a letter to the Cardinal of Venice from the Emperor himself. And for me had muttered an indiscretion.

Our Military Governor General Gorzkowski's heavy hand was no longer approved. Vienna wished to embrace the Empire's people, and not punish them. Gorzkowski would be eased sideways for a while.

"We'll submit a written report," I said. "Let them mull it overnight. Await their summons."

ANA ROVIGO

Snow had stopped and lay in places, and the gaslights had come on. I walked to the quay. There was a last gleam of day beyond the Giudecca.

I smiled, knowing a secret that the few people and the gondolier did not.

I was sorry now for the man I had killed, but he had been arrogant even for them.

And they are not at ease here, I thought. The city is too subtle for them, and in their hearts they would be rid of it, but aren't sure how.

VON ALTDORF

Later, I went for an hour to the old Contessa's weekly evening, where her little greyhounds wandered about like the ones in the old frescoes. The English art critic was there, with his red-haired wife, and I spoke to a man who owned one of the city's beet-sugar refineries, to an opera singer, and to a decrepit but courtly homosexual who said that centuries ago his family had supplied the Republic with two Doges.

The Contessa herself is eighty-six years old and as a girl entered a convent. When this was shut down by Bonaparte she returned to the family palazzo, took a gambler (since dead) as her lover, and now cheats at cards herself, and tells wild tales.

Back in the Danieli, as Franz tugged off my boots, I said "How do you feel?" and he said "Homesick" and I said "So am I."

BASTARDINO

That night the English school party came again to the restaurant, and at once admired the orchids, which Signora Boss had placed on the counter of the cash desk. They were a gift from a satisfied friend, she told them, and they supposed she meant a customer.

Gino said that the sexy English teacher looked even more unhappy, which made her even more sexy.

MARJORIE

Jeff's dinner discussion caught everyone off-guard because it was about modern Venice. Its freak survival. The pressure it was under. How after the last financial crash the Italian government had put a modern real-estate value on all state-owned historic sites, the things visitors come to see, as though they could be sold off and the money put to use.

"Knock down city walls, say, and make space for developers."

"Venice doesn't have walls," said someone.

"The water," said Jeff.

"What?"

"A bigger port. Bigger ships. Bigger factories."

"Skyscrapers." I was surprised to hear myself say. "Economic growth."

"Corrupt contracts with Organised Crime," said the boy who knew about Ziani.

Half of them half-believed conspiracy theories, of course. It's on the web so it must be true.

"Never mind that for the moment," said Jeff. "Just ask yourselves. If what fascinates us is the spirit of a place and we want to experience the energy that created it …"

Celia made a farting noise.

"… But if it's just a museum full of tourists," persisted Jeff, "how can what we see be real?"

Which set them off.

And plump Mrs Wigley said "I often wonder, you know, what's real and what isn't, I mean …"

All I wanted was to get back to England.

BASTARDINO

After the restaurant I sat up with Julia and she told me how lonely she was since her Mother died, and I told her about Maria and wanting to buy a parrot and she said "I know her father's shop. Very posh. Bring her round here for me to meet."

Which made me sleep really well. No surprise, really, after the alley and Old Oysterface's chair.

In the morning Julia woke early for the bakery and then I got up and we had a coffee together and I said "I tell you what. For my Mum and our Dad. Let's go in the dark one morning and collect the leaves and you can make the pies."

"Brilliant," she said. "Do you know a boatman?"

"I think Gino has another cousin," I said.

VON ALTDORF

Gorzkowski is a huge man and his padded dressing-gown made him even bigger. He had a towel over his head and inhaled balsam fumes. Breakfast had not been cleared, an orderly stood behind him and a valet hovered in the dressing-room beyond. Von Baumgarten, high-born and in his depths, I suspect, convinced that Gorzkowski was just another wild Polish careerist, stared at his own fingernails.

Gorzkowski made throaty noises, and waved his arms. The orderly lifted the towel.

My report, I saw, was jam-smeared.

"Ha!" said Gorzkowski. "Colonel. Your report on this Kollbach mishap. Penetrating. But best shelved, don't you think? Entire incident best forgotten?"

"Excellency," I said, and clicked my heels.

"Hell of a woman, though. Make anyone want to fuck her."

His face was wet with steam. He wiped it with his napkin.

"But not what we want to see repeated," he said. "Any opinion on that?"

His arm waved again. The orderly took the napkin.

"Prevention, Excellency, would be entirely a matter of money," said von Baumgarten.

Gorzkowski looked at me.

I did not deny it.

He sighed and nodded.

"Very well," he said. "More money."

Then he offered me a coffee and accepting it I wondered if even the waiter in Florian's was real, or had been invented by Mauerbach.

MARJORIE

From the vaporetto on the way to the airport we saw a flotilla of gondolas and realised that it was some part of Cassandra's mother's Uncoupling, because the celebrant, a chaplet of flowers on her head, stood at the prow and what must have been the mother, and a head-slumped Cassandra herself, sat behind her.

"They're all mad," said James Parker. "She texts us. Her father never even showed up."

"What?" said Jeff.

"He just paid to get rid of them, Sir."

"The Doge," said Jeff, "chucking the ring into the sea."

I looked at the receding city and managed not to weep and Charlene, who had lost her phone, said "It's all right, Miss, I know how you feel."

POSTCARD OF THE PIAZZA SAN MARCO SENT BY ONE OF THE BOYS TO HIS SISTER
X marks spot where we fed pigeons and one shat on your friend Celia's arm ha ha I hate you

POSTCARD OF A GONDOLA AND OARSMAN SENT BY
ONE OF THE BOYS TO HIS GRANDMOTHER
Dear Gran, We're in Venice which is amazing. You would love it.
Sending this to the hospital because Mum says you're still there.
Get well soon. Love.

POSTCARD OF GIORGIONE'S 'LA TEMPESTA' SENT BY
ONE OF THE GIRLS TO HER PARENTS. SHE DID NOT
HAVE AN ITALIAN STAMP AND POSTED IT AT
HEATHROW ON THE WAY HOME
Best trip ever. Made up my mind. Want to take History of Art at
Uni. Love you. xxxx

MARJORIE

In Wolverhampton once I went on a dating app encounter and he
was nothing like his photo, had a ridiculous brown wig and
talked about stamp collecting. But I was afraid to look at any of
the sites now, and afraid to see Dad in case he noticed my defeat.
But I could not put it off, and found him alone at the bus stop.

"Where's Mr Woodward, then? Caught the ferry?"

"Yes," said Dad, and my attempted joke was tactless because
during one of the nights I was away Mr Woodward had
collapsed. A low potassium level. He died in the ambulance, and
Dad did not criticize me. He thought I was Mum and said Did
she know that Marjorie was in Venice? Good for her. Not sure
when she's back. Maybe she won't be.

In Common Room breaks I no longer knew what to say to
colleagues. I just saw hair in the men's nostrils and thought how
crude they were. So I would sit near Jeff who reads his paper
amid the chatter and one day he turned a page and said "My
word!" and looked at me.

"What?"

"Ziani."

"What?"

"Assassinated. They found his body."

I was blank.

"You remember, don't you?"

"No."

"We talked about him. Venice. The political blogger."

"Oh ..." I said.

He read part of the report but I did not listen. I could not wait to get on my tablet and order more cheap clothes to see what difference they could make.

None. So at another lunch hour I took them to a charity shop and when I returned one of the school secretaries said "There's someone asked for you."

"Who?"

"Not a parent. I think she's foreign. She's in the front car park."

I went out. No-one. I looked round. A taxi, door ajar. She stepped out.

I envied her. The aplomb. The leather-trimmed alpaca jacket. The little lace-up shoes.

"Miss Marjorie?"

"Yes."

"Then I find you."

"I'm sorry, but I –"

She held out a fist. I opened my palm. She dropped something into it.

A ring.

I tried to breathe. My eyes stung.

I heard Jeff's voice, that before I had blocked out.

"... traced by hacking his mobile phone ... abducted from a hotel, it is thought ... identified by a signet ring because his real name was ..."

"I know," I said. "I'm sorry. I just ..."

"You were the woman of his life," she said. "So he took the risk. It can happen like that, I suppose."

My tears obscured her elegance.

"Are you his wife?" I said.

"No, no. I'm Ana."

She kissed me, resolutely, and returned to the taxi, and it drove away. We're about half an hour from Heathrow, after all. Inside the building a bell rang.

I do want to be a teacher, I thought, because I now have something to say. I will withdraw my resignation.

He had died because of me, and I felt shocked and marvellous. I put the ring on my finger and the city rose from the water, the clouds were a fresco, the patrollers and patricians fixed in their poses. We will all die and be forgotten, I thought. Why is it that they are not?

THE END

9 780957 182950